I0670647

Pink Flamingo Waves

(A Collection of Seven Short Stories)

Written by P.G. Neil

"Pink Flamingo Waves," by P.G. Neil. ISBN 978-1-951985-84-4 (softcover); 978-1-951985-85-1 (eBook).

Published 2021 by Virtualbookworm.com Publishing, P.O. Box 9949, College Station, TX 77842, US. © 2021, P.G. Neil. All rights reserved.
No part of this publication may be reproduced, stored in a retrieval system, or transmitted in any form or by any means, electronic, mechanical, recording or otherwise, without the prior written permission of P.G. Neil.

The Stories

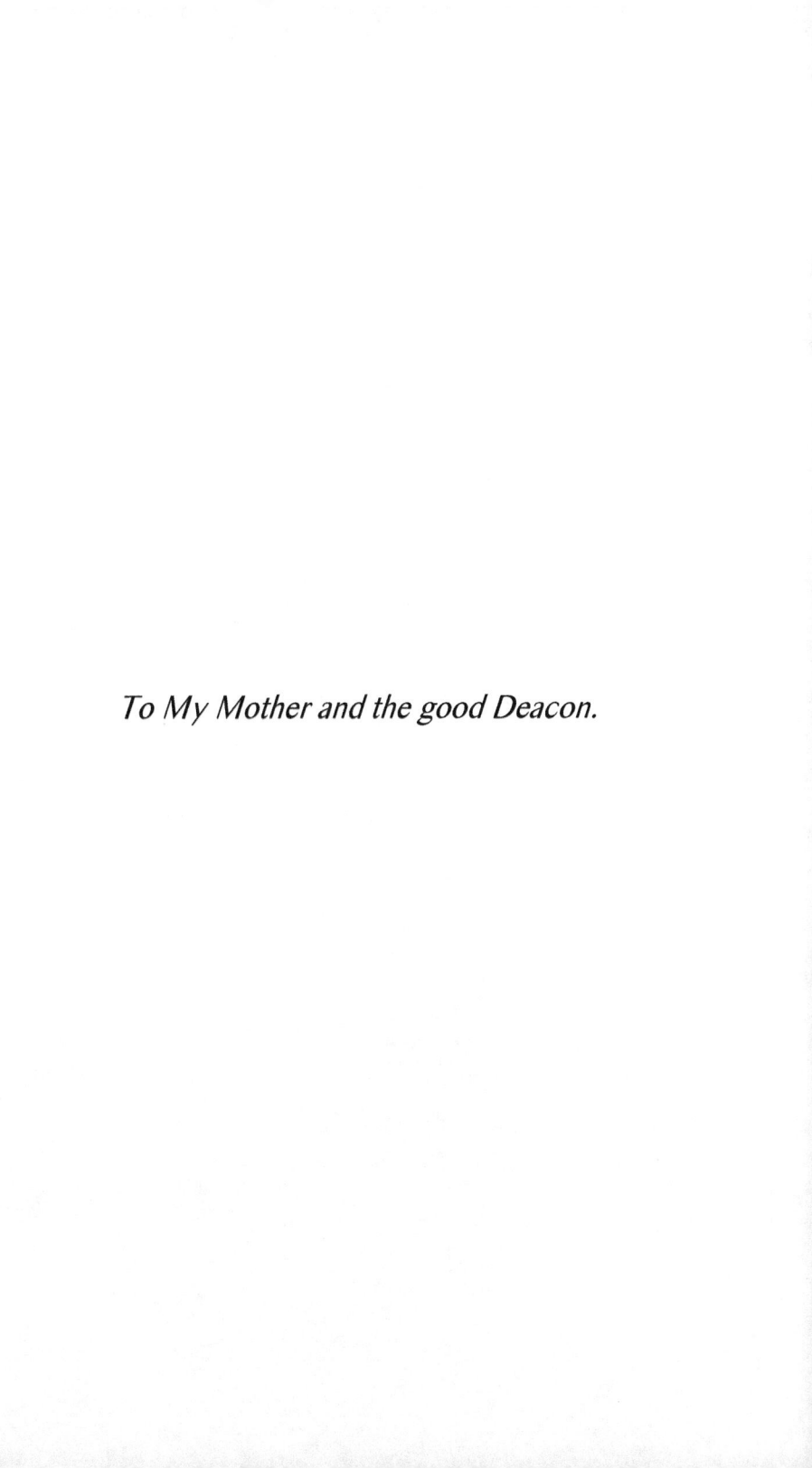

To My Mother and the good Deacon.

The Motherless

I.

Baking under the sun is the sand of Surfrider Beach, staking out my Turf. Or should I say my adopted turf, as I look out, I see waves crash around the expert surfers riding them. Most of the surfers are locals however we don't have to broadcast it, though. I could and get shamed for it, but there's no point in disclosure. To have one of the best surf breaks in the world in your backyard is nothing to take for granted. I never liked the locals that monopolized the Malibu waves. I've seen guns pulled out, beat downs, and ego confrontations from Topanga to Zeros, sending the same message, Locals Only! That's something I'm fortunate to be aware of, but not involved in. Too many guys lack that awareness, and like riding a wave, they reach heights only to crash and never recover. No principles to help them back up, no glory, only self-reflected ego. It all comes down to respect and relationships. Never ride another person's wave, especially when they've been out all day waiting for it. This point is driven home by the burning sand under my bare, tan feet. I considered myself used to this, which makes me wonder how the newbies tolerate it. I imagine it's like hot coals for them, but it is a badge of honor for us experienced riders. Not a place you'd want to lay your head and not a place you'd want to fall, but pride will see to it that you do. As I gaze down at my turquoise Birdwell Britches, I wonder how the Chumash felt about this sand.

My squinted eyes shift from the ocean to my best friend, Travis walking beside me. The sun is beaming down on him just as much as it is me, so I know he can't see me looking at him from the side of his squinted eyes fixated on the waves we approach ahead. Or maybe he's focused on the babes in their two pieces, fantasying about the ultimate goal of penetration. Whatever he is seeing doesn't change what I see when I look at him, pride and honor. I always ponder on the efforts I make to help him see things as I do. Not that I'm perfect, I just know I can help him. I don't come off preachy because he'd detect that and detest me. Or maybe he already knows what I'm up to when I try to steer him toward better choices discreetly. Perhaps he knows my intent and puts up with it because it's coming from me. Maybe he knows I'm there for him whether he changes or not. If that's what he thinks, then he's right. The streets probably made him smarter than I give him credit for. He's probably two steps ahead of me at every turn. I mean, I grew up in a trailer park in Santa Fe, New Mexico. Travis grew up in a ten-million-dollar villa off the cliffs of the Encinal bluffs. However, he would've preferred the trailer park rather than the pretentious drudgery of life. We're the same age, but his soul is older than mine.

II.

I'm an only child, and so is Travis which made us brothers. This may be the only real thing we shared in common when we first met. We were also connected by music and our love for surfing and listening to the Eagles. It was just Travis and his father until his father met his twenty-three-year-old fiancée who he jet-sets around the world. Tilda. She's the reason Paul neglects Travis, which has created a rift that Travis barriers in his soul. She's the reason the streets of downtown LA raised Travis and caused him to escape.

We're closer to the water now as the mist hit my face and the sun caused are eyes to squint. Travis whoops as we approach the crashing waves with our surfboards. He started on shortboards, but I've convinced him that single fin longboards are the only way. Miki Dora was right, the aesthetic feel of riding along small waves is unmatched with a much longer ride quality.

Travis has come to love the single-fin culture so much that he bought me a 9'9 Gato Heroi 'Creme' board for my birthday. He didn't even look at the price, but knew that I would love it. Actually it might be a sign of resentment as he just swiped his father's American Express card. He throws up a hand in greeting toward the direction of a young crowd. He's pretty popular around here, too, even though I'm the one pursuing a career as a pro surfer. Travis doesn't need to be popular, he knows what he is. Being popular would never satisfy the soul of a guy like Travis, just the waves and only the waves. He doesn't need the money as I do, which makes him free.

Maggie, my Mother, works two jobs, and she has for a while now. Ever since I was a kid she would be gone all day sometimes working three jobs. That's how she was able to support me. I think about my Mother all the time. I wonder if her life would have been better if she wouldn't have had me at such an early age. My father was afraid to face the music and ran out on her as soon as she told him she was pregnant. Travis had money and resources but was utterly oblivious with no direction. He was more miserable than I was, as the lazy days started to pile up on one another. Despite that difference, our lives today hold more resemblance than they did back when we first met. I credit my Mother for cultivating my Christian faith allowing me to see the big picture. It's made me a better person and has given me hope. A commitment I vowed to fulfil six months ago when she got baptized with me at Will Rogers Beach (Tower 4), to be exact. She took the Southwestern Chief to Union Station to get dipped in the Pacific with me. A beach baptism what could be better? My Mother is a lovely person!

Contrary to widespread belief, you don't get dipped and suddenly come up with a changed person. I didn't and at first I felt like I did something wrong. From time to time, I find myself wrestling with my old demons, specifically the Santa Fe demons. They find a way to keep up with me no matter how hard I resist, so maybe they aren't that old. Their vitality seems to equal mine at times. Perhaps it's what keeps me in shape and gives me my fighting spirit that I manifest in sexual relationships with the many beach babes. Maybe the same goes for Travis and his demons. We're both about as lean as our surfboards, toned muscles calling for sex. His tanned obliques are a little more well defined than mine, though. Plus, he's a natural blonde with the 'surfer look.' I'm dark-haired and dark skinned - there used to be a derogatory term for my type back in the Miki Dora days, but I don't recollect the name. The negative stigma of being Hispanic didn't become apparent to me until I moved to California. My estranged father was of Irish descent, but I positively identified with my Hispanic blood since I was raised with my Mother's side. I also took my Mother's maiden name, "Cortez."

For this reason, I'm convinced I have the stronger demons than Travis. My past as a member of a gang while I lived in Santa Cruz, New Mexico, just north of Santa Fe during my early teens, is what haunts me. We called ourselves "Los DesMadres" or 'The Motherless' although I'm not sure if that's the proper translation. We just stole stuff—a lot of stuff. Mom tells me that God is the creator of the universe and forgives all sins. I'm still a work in progress, but I hope she's right as I need forgiveness. Travis only listens to LA gangster rap, which is a pet peeve of mine. I can appreciate gangster rap, but I find it more exhilarating to listen to East Coast hip hop from the '90s. I've tried turning him on to A Tribe Called Quest, but he's so set in his ways. Not sure his taste in music is changing anytime soon, but that's the least of his problems as far as I'm concerned. Anyway, we both love The Eagles, so that's all that matters. He is selling drugs and pursuing dirty money that I want him to be done with. His ties to the streets of downtown LA might be too deep for him to break away from. Maybe my links to the streets through Travis are too deep, but today we're in Malibu, and it's a beautiful day, so I'm not too worried.

III.

Something grabbed Travis' attention like a thief in the night, and then it caused me to spring up. A commotion broke out in the mixed crowd, two boys were involved in an altercation—turf wars. I take off across the hot sand as I would feel responsible if someone got hurt. I don't know every soul on the beach, but I know the sound of feet sifting through sand behind me is Travis. He always has my back and we were on our way.

A We each weighed around one-fifty, and one of these guys quickly looked to be about two- hundred pounds. I start to pull them apart but suddenly feel dizzy. At the same time, I realize my hearing has returned when I feel a burning sensation across my back. I was caught across the jaw with a punch before I knew what hit me—knocked out for a few seconds. Travis is already in both their faces, with his finger pointed between one of the boys' eyes. This is probably the one who hit me, but I wanted to handle this. I get up and moved between Travis and the surfers. I'm so angry that the hot sand feels cool.

"Fuck! What the fuck is wrong with you idiots?!"

One blames the other.

"Kelly fucking Slater over here dropped in on me. Almost took my eye out!"

Before I could alleviate the situation, the other surfer's eyes widened as he stared at me with a sudden realization before blurting out,

"Oh shit! Cortez!!"

I try to control my temper, but the first thought through my mind wouldn't be silenced.

"How do I know this guy?"

"How does he know my last name?"

The second thought was that I must have sold him weed or something. Before I could say anything, Travis' body slams the other surfer to the ground. This is the one who hit me. Travis is more robust than he looks, and I sometimes wonder if his demons are more with him than they are against him. He picks up a surfboard and breaks it over the boy's leg then proceeds to lecture him,

"If I ever see you here again, you're fucking dead,"

The boy lies in agony. Blood running down his leg. The other surfer runs off.

"You didn't have to break his board."

Travis is still cooling down from the adrenaline rush.

"He fucking hit you in the face. Nobody hits my boy in the face like that."

"I appreciate the gesture, but they're just kids. We did the same shit at that age."

Travis picks up his board to signify that he's already moved on,

"Whatever, man. Let's hit it!"

I watch him take off for the waves as he splatters through the water. I pick up my board and take off after him. Later that night, Travis and I decided it was time to get out of Malibu for a few days. All the tourists were coming in for Labor Day weekend, so the PCH turned into a parking lot.

"Let's go down to Kilometer 38," Travis says.

I respond, "Fuck, Mexico?"

Billy Joe Shaver wrote a song called, "Ain't No God in Mexico," performed by the great Waylon Jennings.

"Ain't no God in Mexico, Ain't no way to understand, how that border crossing feeling makes a fool out of a man."

However, the waves were heavenly this time of year near Kilometer 38 - a break just south of Tijuana in Baja California. If you went further down to deep Baja, we could catch some great waves on longboards near Scorpion Bay (San Juanico), but we didn't have the time to go that far down. We brought a longboard just in case and were ready to go at a minute's notices. Waves just kept rolling in at K38 this time of year. One after another, all day long like the rhythm of a heartbeat. It's heaven I recalled thinking. Travis had some business partners he knew down there. The Suarez brothers. I know, sounds like a couple of characters out of the movie Scarface. Well, these two were similar characters to that of the film. Drug dealer's Travis met through his downtown LA connections. I acquiesced in my decision.

"Fuck it, let's go! It's beautiful down there," I said.

Plus, we could drink wine down in the Valle de Guadalupe (Basically the Napa Valley of Mexico). Only one problem. I hadn't read or seen the news in Mexico lately.

IV.

Glass bottles are being thrown at Mexican Naval officers on the dark streets of Tijuana. Some over signs held by protesters reading 'Free Angel.' The characters fall as the officers engage the crowd with batons. The streetlights, combined with the mist of tear gas, creates a blanket of fog over the chaos on Calle Revolution, It's all a blur. The only thing it can't distort are the piercing sounds of whistles and the screams of protesters being beaten. A path is cleared for an anxious camera crew following a man in shackles surrounded by guards armed with Heckler and

MP5 submachine guns. The cameraman slows his pace and walks peacefully alongside the stoic guards now that he's found a right angle on Angel Suarez, who wears leg irons on his way to the black SUV waiting up ahead. His dark eyebrows are thick like the hair on the back of his cuffed hands. The chaos is drowned out momentarily by the whirring blades of two BO-105 helicopters that begin to hover over the area. The cameraman tries to keep the reporter beside him in a frame as the path grows narrower the closer, they get to the black SUV. She holds a heavy microphone in one hand and covers her ear with the other as she shouts over the roaring helicopters.

"Authorities have captured Angel Suarez here in Tijuana this afternoon. Angel is accused of more than three-hundred murders. Once he split from the infamous Concepcion Cartel, Suarez continued to operate a drug trafficking organization in and around Tijuana. Tuesday arrest was the result of more than five months of intelligence operations. There was a reward of up to thirty million pesos, 2.4 million dollars for the capture of Angel Suarez,"

She finishes just in time as the guards put Angel in the back of the SUV. The door slams behind him, and it drives off. The camera crew's attention shifts to a man they couldn't see until now. The man behind the SUV. Behind the state of chaos, Tijuana is in. Miguel Calderon the DEA agent is responsible for Angel Suarez's arrest appears. He's in the center of a group of other DEA agents, well protected from the protesters who hate his guts. I'm cleaning up the streets of Tijuana, he thought which justified his crack down. His focus was on the big men on the streets, the ones you don't mess with, the ones that spark riots when they disappear. Those were the only ones Calderon had an interest in. Those cases brought him the most attention and no matter how terrible things looked on the outside, secretly he loved the attention that came with controversy. His appetite is never satisfied, and his desire to pursue the "bad guy" justified his own evils. Cracking a case like this is a rarity and perhaps the only reason he broke this one is that he is a distant relative of the Suarez family. This, too, is kept a secret from the public. Calderon recalls the story of his great grandfather Candido. In 1910, the latter married Angelica Suarez in a traditional Mexican wedding at the La Paloma Chapel, just down the hill from the Cristo del Sagrado Corazo statue. To this day, rumor has it that after finding out that Candido had cheated on her after only two years of marriage, Angelica tried to take the lives of her children and herself but was unsuccessful in doing so. Candido found her with a gun drawn on their youngest daughter. Before she could pull the trigger, Candido shot and killed his wife. The tragic story has always lingered around the small town and was the only actual proof that few had when discussing the distant relations between Calderon and the Suarez family. Today Calderon is hailed as a hero in Tijuana, and the Suarez drug cartel is slowly becoming obsolete.

V.

He makes eye contact with the reporter and waves her in as she approaches. This was a cue for the agents around him to make room for her. He knows she wasn't going to wait for permission. His story is what the media thrives on, hate! Perhaps he just has a thing for blue-eyed blondes. His crooked smile would suggest so as he looked at her with lust. His pride might suggest otherwise since he wastes no time snatching the microphone away from the pretty reporter before she can get a question out.

"He is one of the most notorious drug lords and was on a list of the top twenty-four traffickers in all of Mexico."

She watches alongside her cameraman, stunned, as Calderon looks directly into the lens and strokes his ego. The people of Tijuana find it hard to believe that Angel Suarez's brother Leo has gone missing. This is the rhetoric Calderon spews into the camera, but it's not news. It's just part of the reason he's hated by many. The Suarez family is in turmoil behind closed doors, but this town's people love them. To the people, Calderon has kicked the Suarez family while they were down. Angel's neutral countenance, despite the circumstances, is a veil. He wears it continuously, and even now, as he approaches La Mesa, his features say nothing. You couldn't tell if he was hopeless or if he already had concrete plans in motion for revenge. Who would he be targeting? Calderon, but who helped him? He thought. The Suarez family is too careful and too connected for Calderon to have done this on his own. It had to be someone close to the family, someone who was like family and has turned. When the name Travis Rose comes to mind, so do ideas for Angel's next move, and for the first time in a long time, emotion visibly escapes Angel's cold exterior as the corner of his mouth rises slightly.

VI.

At the Mexican border checkpoint, a patrol officer gestures for Travis and me to drive right through.

"That was easy," I say as he accelerates.

"Getting in is the easy part. It's getting out that's difficult."

Travis says.

"We're in fucking Mexico!"

I laugh at Travis' reaction as it's the same every time. I'm usually the reserved one, which is why his brow furrowed when I shouted. I'm just trying to keep the tone light. Things were tense when he first told me that Angel called him after being arrested. Things were more than tense, as they were filled with angst. After all, we were never really coming down here for the surf. Travis has this all planned out from the get-go. I brought me along for back since I was Hispanic (we'll only half), but I nevertheless looked the part. Luckily, I was the sober one and was smart enough to know that coming down here after finding out the real reason why we came down was a terrible idea. That's when I snapped as I was reminded of how short my temper was, but by that time, I had already rushed him, and we were already exchanging blows like enemies.

I just thought he was fucking insane for coming to Mexico to get money from one of the Suarez brothers after the other was just locked up. In no way am I a hundred percent okay with this, but I wasn't going to let him come here alone even if he is convinced that Angel has his back. I don't believe much loyalty exists in the streets, especially these streets, but Angel loved Travis, or so I thought, so I figured everything would be okay. When I pressed him on this, it only made matters worse, but what could be worse than being in debt to a family that runs a drug cartel? I realized that was Travis, my best friend. Somebody entangled in a coil of street favors always pushing the envelope. Supposedly there's money in this for Travis a lot, but I don't see why he needs it. It was never about the money for him anyway, only the thrill of not getting caught. We shouldn't be here, but it was either both of us or neither of us. I notice his eyes squinting as if the sun were in them as we cruise down the empty road. The dash reads 1:06 AM, so it must be the dust in the air that's burning his eyes. Or maybe he's hiding something. Perhaps he's not sure of how things will go once he meets Leo face to face. He's probably downplaying the danger of it all. If he's lying, that makes two of us. I haven't shaken the guilt I feel for telling my Mother I was coming here to surf with Travis. I told her in the church of all places.

On top of that, I was late, so bearing the news of this trip made it easy for me to bite my tongue when she scolded me. I knew I would be making things a little harder for her. A lump form in my throat just thinking about her. She was singing with her eyes closed when I discreetly moved down the pew to sit beside her. When she finally sat down, she opened her bible and leaned into me with her finger following the text as our pastor read it. Just like she did when I was a kid. We have the same brown eyes and dark hair. The most significant difference in her tone is pale compared to mine, but at 62, her features are still like a 30-year-old. We did have Sicilian ancestry, maybe it was the

Mediterranean paternal grandmother I never met. She only goes out for work and keeps leisure time short. She likes her red wine. That must be her secret to youth, along with her faith. Her only demon was my father, and he's long gone.

VII.

I lose my train of thought when Travis blares the horn at some dogs in the street, It's road rage. The dogs scatter into the shadows as the sound pierces the cold night air. Travis' wrist is slung back over the wheel as his Rolex glistens under the dim street lights. It was a graduation gift from his father, a sign of who he was. The moment was unusual but didn't last long before Tilda appeared like a temptress with whispers and dragged Paul away. It was something about a flight this time and I imagine Travis has taken note of her timing. The way she always comes in between them. I wouldn't trust her any more than the dark corners of this town. At first, I was concerned because I forgot my visa, but Travis assured me that border patrol wouldn't ask for it unless we were more than 150 miles inland. He said we weren't going that far. Our motel is in Rosarito, a beautiful paradise where you can buy a beach house overlooking the Pacific for less than $100,000 here. K-38 is a beautiful reef, and epic scenery. The wind hits it from the East all the groundswells. We often considered trying to buy one when Travis' dad offered to lend us the money since we loved coming down here to surf, the point. When you don't know where you are, everything sounds far. That's where my mind was... lost. This isn't my first visit to Mexico, but even though Travis and I frequented K38, he shared my broad eyed expression as we both took in Revolution Blvd as if for the first time. For him, a lot must have changed and for me, the beggar women with their babies, cantinas, and strip joints were all a first. Whores are abundant so fucking was not an issue. Some with sunken eyes and missing teeth, **but who needs teeth? (This is funny lol**). Miles of businesses aimed at Americans' daily visits are draped with a compendium of transnational, corporate advertising billboards.

Travis' phone rings as we pull into the lot of an old, adobe stone motel.

"It's Leo!"

He says to me as he frantically jumps out of the truck to take a call.

"We're in Rosarito right now."

His anxious tone shifts into questioning,

"Is it on the main strip?"

He asks while looking up and down the road.

"Okay, see you then."

He gets back in and starts the engine.

"We're going to meet Leo,"

he says looking over his shoulder, already in reverse.

"Can't you wait until tomorrow? Let's just crash man."

I know my words are falling on deaf ears, Travis is in business mode. His eyes are on the sign ahead, taking us onto the Mexico 1D. The speedometer reads 55 as the speed increases. Ironically as we enter the trans peninsular highway, a convoy of police vehicles with sirens drive swiftly back towards town. This is Kilometer 38 and I can only imagine the crazy shit that goes on here. As we were both finally able to eat something, we pulled over to the taco stand before hitting some waves, The Pink Flamingo Waves. We would call them pink flamingo waves any time we surfed filthy waves in retrospect to Travis's favorite movie Pink Flamingos.

VIII.

I wipe my eyes and see Leo catch a wave. He surfs like a legend, with so much confidence and grace that his perfect balance puts the anxious lifeguards at ease. However, there aren't any "Sam Elliot" type lifeguards here. These were private Mexican lifeguards who would be executed if anything happened to Suarez. Somehow, they were allowed on Rosarito's beach, but I guess it was Suarez's beach. They own this territory, and that's how it is. I joked with Leo when we met last night, suggesting he held all of Mexico. A modest grin under his piercing green eyes is all that he replied with. He's 21 but looks older than that. His demons probably overpower easily given the lifestyle he lives. His build is average, not toned like mine or Travis. I break away from Travis and Leo to find the hollow section of a break and float in the tube-like barrel until the wave forces me to go back out onto the open face, which is like a crystal in the sunlight. I follow Leo and Travis, who spin hang-tens off of their single-fin longboards.

"One- fin, One- God" - like the saying goes. Their brotherly bond doesn't bother me, and it won't as long as it lasts until we leave this place.

For now, I'm enjoying the moment. Surfers and onlookers alike are having fun in the sun- splashed, Mexican Riviera waters. The beauty of nature caused everyone to forget about the blood that must have spilled across this sand! I found it odd that Leo kept looking at his phone while the three of us waiting for our food at the taco stand. Travis doesn't seem to notice, probably because he's just been handed three carne asada tacos, of course all for himself. With his appetite, I'm surprised he didn't get more. I take my food next, then Leo's tray comes up and his phone rings. Travis grabs the tray for Leo, who covertly walks away to answer it. We find an empty bench. Travis is already down to one taco. I sit, and my first bite is during Travis' last.
My brows furrow.

"Seriously?"

I say, wondering how he eats so fast. He gesticulates to Leo's tacos before checking over his shoulder. We both laugh as Leo makes his way toward us.

"I don't know what the fuck is so funny. That was Angel on the phone. He wants us to go to La Mesa (One of Mexico's worst prisons) and visit him right now."

If Travis entered a mode when it came to serious business, it pales in comparison to Leo's, who looks like he'd kill us if we refused, so I get up with no questions asked.

IX.

Was it that look in Leo's eyes that granted us access to La Mesa prison? I wondered. Was the mode he was in? The officer at the guard shack waved us in like we were dinner guests, meeting the King. A path was cleared as we rode in. We were even greeted by several guards and some inmates in the yard. Even Travis seemed to be in a different state of mind. Not the mode he was in before, but pensive. Like something could go wrong at any minute. It's like he knew exactly what his role was even though he told me he didn't. He didn't ask questions when Leo decided to drive; he just handed over the keys. Leo's face is why we've been welcomed here like family. Not even the guards in the tower looking down at us for very long. The guard escorting us inside doesn't speak as we pass the visitors' line in the sally port. Most of them are women with children. The guard shows his face through the small window beside a solid steel door.

A loud buzzer blared before it was opened. I'm jolted out of my train of thought, and anxiety runs across my body. I look at Travis, who seems calm. How? My palms are beginning to sweat. He's in deeper than he says, and I know that something is up. He must be if he's this relaxed, I thought. I follow behind them on high alert. I notice Leo reaching into his right jacket pocket as we approach a guard who sits at a desk. My eyes are locked on his hand until he removes it. I see money, but how much? He slips it to the guard who doesn't seem concerned about being noticed.

Who would reprimand him? Leo runs this place. Why did Leo even bother sliding it across the desk discreetly? Another loud buzzer startles me even though my eyes were already watching the steel door in front of us. This buzzer brings my Mother to mind; fear comes over me as we walk through it. What would happen if I was locked up in prison in Mexico so far from Maggie? Her heart would break. I would cause her pain greater than my worthless father. A lump begins to form in my throat. I regret leaving every time I think of her, but I can't let that show now. I scratch my forehead even though it doesn't itch to distract myself and detract any glares from noticing my watery eyes. I can't wipe them. Or can I? A large roach scatters by me, showing the true disrepair we were in. I walk funny to avoid crushing it, causing me to stand out. Leo looks back, somehow knowing that something was off with me. I maintain a principled facade well enough to convince him that there wasn't. His eyes leave me and with them goes the fear they imposed. I hate roaches, but that was the distraction I needed. Travis doesn't turn around, just keeps moving like a machine. He's pretty much a robot—the door slams behind us. The loudness of this place annoys me. We wait in a lobby with rusted walls, and the tile beneath our feet is plagued with web-like cracks. Probably where the roaches hide.

Above us are bare bulbs that are dirty somehow. Leo impatiently checks his watch and a nervous guard, armed with a machine gun, runs out to meet us. Judging by how Leo yells at him, he must be late, but it's all in Spanish, so that I couldn't know for sure. I can imagine Leo is someone who you don't keep waiting, not even for a second. The guard bows and runs over to a wall with a remote in hand. He pushes buttons, and part of the wall slides open. Leo proceeds without another word to the guard, and we follow him into a narrow hallway leading to a private suite.

X.

I felt awkward watching Travis and Leo greeting Angel with hugs, but relieved at the same time. It was nice to see the tension broken. Angel ran this place like a king. Two pretty women in their 20's served us coffee and Mexican danishes. I didn't shy away from indulging, fuck it were on vacation I thought. A hunger came over me when I laid eyes on the Mexican pastries. Suddenly it felt like I hadn't eaten in days. I didn't fill my mouth all at once, even though no one else seemed interested in the food.

"Not a bad man. When you called and told me you got arrested, I thought they locked you up under the jail. How do you get this? How does this work?" Travis asked.

"I bought it. This one costs eighty grand, and there's only four or five like this. Some vato came in and paid a hundred and ten."

This piqued Travis' interest even more.

"You don't pay rent?"

"No, no, I own it. I can sell it too as long as comandante gets his cut. They got others that cost anywhere from ten grand up. We own a few, don't we Leonardo?"

"Yeah, what the fuck, we're real estate investors in the penitentiary."

I would join in on the laughter if my mouth weren't full. Travis hasn't noticed that I took his danish.

"Angel, this is my friend Trip."

I quickly wipe my hands to shake Angel's.

"What do you think of La Mesa?"

"It's not bad. You could probably get out of here if you wanted to?"

I say, swallowing the last of my danish.

"Oh yeah, the warden would hold the ladder up for me. I pay him ten grand a month to feed his kids. That's about fifteen times his salary."

I try not to appear too shocked. The women bring us more coffee and pastries.

"Speaking of which, that's what I brought you fellas in here to talk about today. Travis, I have a job for you."

"What kind of job?" Travis asks.

"I need you to take care of an enemy for me. The bastard that put me in this mess. Miguel Calderon."

"You mean like take care of him, take care of him?" Travis asks.

"I mean, like crucify the son of a bitch and make him suffer."

I jump in for clarity.

"You mean you want him to kill him?"

"No one, I want both of you to kill him."

I maintain composure while contemplating how to get out of here with Travis, who interjects,

"Bro, you told me to come down here to pick up the money you owed me. You said a small favor."

Angel smirks before his response,

"This is a small favor compared to your reward. You and your vato are a safe bet for an alibi. We already have this thing figured out."

"Who's we?" Travis asks.

Leo responds, "You're doing us a favor here that will never be discounted and you two will go back home with more than that hundred grand we owe you."

"How much more?" Travis asks.

"One million dollars," Leo says, confident that Travis won't refuse.

XI.

Miguel Calderon sits alone at a bar in Tijuana. He's one of the last patrons, and it's evident that he's been drinking all night. He and the bartender have become friends. The American jazz in the background sets the tone for the confession Calderon has brewing inside. The bartender pours him another tequila,

"The last one's on me, hero."

Calderon sees the clock behind the counter reads 5:01 AM.

"I'm no hero. I'm just as much a criminal as they are."

The bartender laughs then responds,

"It takes one to know one."

Calderon responds in a slur "I'm serious. I'm evil."

"Anyone that puts the Suarez brothers behind bars is a hero in my book."

Calderon blurts out his words,

"I'm related to the Suarez brothers. Didn't know that did you?"

The bartender's expression is drawn to convince the drunkard that he's surprised, even though he isn't. Somehow, this isn't news to him.

"You're kidding!"

A full-on act by the bartender ensues. Calderon is unable to detect the facade as he continues his confession.

"You want to hear some crazy shit?"

The bartender leans in for information as the last patron leaves him alone with the intoxicated DEA agent.

XII.

I waited until Travis and I were alone before I snapped at him. It didn't escalate into a brawl, but that's because Leo's mansion, like a hacienda, was crawling with armed guards (similar to that of the character Alejandro Sosa's Hacienda in the movie Scarface - another similarity) and deep down, I knew there was no way out of this. I also suspected that Leo wasn't far, which meant he would hear us if I shouted so I kept my cool. A warmth runs through my head, it's what I'd feel whenever I experienced defeat, only this time I didn't know exactly what I was losing. Maybe I haven't lost it yet. Maybe myself is what I'm losing. I feel like a slave, like I'm trapped, helpless, oppressed. As I sit across from Travis at the dining room table, I'm forced to accept the reality that Leo has us under his control and there's nothing either of us can do about it. I know I can't function like this, so I let the smell of chorizo and eggs take my mind off of the betrayal I feel by the man I once called my best friend. Then I discovered Angelica Suarez - their 19-year-old sister preparing our breakfast. I would stare a hole into Travis' if his eyes were not avoiding mine. I watch Angelica instead as she gracefully removes homemade tortillas from the oven. I didn't notice when we were introduced last night, but everything she does is graceful; I was too angry to pay attention, but knew I wanted to Fuck her. Instead of letting the smell of food clear my mind, I let her do it. She's beautiful and carefree, the perfect distraction. She dances to the corrido music playing as she serves us. Her fragrance must've captivated Travis when she poured the orange juice in his cup because he's watching her now too. Judging by his slacked jaw, she must look completely different than she did when Travis last saw her three years ago. My eyes are witnessing her caramel complexion and long dark hair for the first time. She knows her body mystifies us as she moves around the room, tending to all culinary preparations. My eyes are locked on her legs even as Leo enters, "Travis!"

He startles out of a trance at the sound of Leo's voice,

"Can I speak to you in private?"

Leo gives me a look as Travis follows him out. It's a look of distrust, but also like that of a jealous boyfriend. That's the only thing that's stood out to me since we've arrived. Leo and Angelica seem to be closer than a brother and sister. It's coming back to me now as she smiles at me. I recognize it from last night. It's the same smile she gave us after Leo called her into his room, only she was almost naked. She had been dancing after dinner and drinking. She started stripping, but it was just Travis and I watching before Leo entered and called her. He gave both of us a look then. A jealous one. I could speculate, but what's the point? What does their relationship have to do with Travis and me? I begin eating.

"The food is delicious," I say.

"They are planning to kill you after you kill Calderon."

Food goes down the wrong pipe, and I nearly choke. She nervously looks across the room at the doorway where Leo and Travis made their exit.

"It's a plan. An alibi." I recover.

"Travis would never do that to me. I've known him my entire life."

"You don't know him as well as you think you do gringo."

It didn't take much for her to convince me of that. My mind is racing, and suddenly I don't know what to believe. She surveys the surroundings before unloading the information.

"Travis and my family go way back. My brothers were raised by Travis' dad when my Mother worked as his nanny up in Malibu."

"What are you talking about?"

"Paul Rose - Travis' dad is a drug dealer and has been since the early 1970s."

"This is fucking crazy. You're crazy; you're fucking lying to me. Why would you tell me this? You don't even know me. They're your brothers. You're choosing me over them?"

I wasn't sure if she was lying. I was more so desperate for the truth.

"Who do you think helps get the drugs from Mexico to the states? My brothers use his boats to do it."

My mind is abandoning me. None of this makes sense even though I want it to.

"I don't want to see anyone die. I need you to help me, so we can both be set free. Otherwise, we both die,"

She says softly. This must be her seductive powers. She's trying to lure me into a trap, I thought,

"You don't even know me,"

I bury my head in my palms and close my eyes. Maybe this will help me think straight. She places a comforting hand on my shoulder.

"I can see everything in your eyes. I know you're a good person."

Something's happening inside me. A warmth. A pull I can't resist, It's her. I look up, and her green eyes lock with mine, and before I could blink, I'm kissing her passionately. This is all insane, I thought but the emotions got me going.

XIII.

The hanging sign is flipped to convey that the bar is closed, but the bartender oddly watches the door anyway—his attention shifts when a glass break. The sun rays hit Calderon's face. He knocked it over while stirring awake.

"Rise and shine." The bartender says while grabbing a broom.

"So, Leo put his brother behind bars. That's some wild shit."

Calderon is confused for a moment, "What'd you say?"

"Did you already forget what you told me before you passed out? Leo put Angel, his brother, behind bars, and he used YOU to do it."

Calderon is hungover and still out of it, "Yeah. True story."

"So, he's fucking his sister and doesn't want Angel to find out about it."

"Angel would kill both of them if he did,"

Calderon passes out again, and the bartender's laugh transitions into silence as his cell phone rings. He answers it, "Yeah?"

Of course, I remember kissing Angelica, but everything else is foggy now that I'm standing in front of an extensive selection of ammunition and gun artillery beside Travis and Leo. They indulge in a pile of cocaine. It's like they're the best friends and I'm the outsider. Angelica is nowhere in sight. Time seems to be moving faster, as I feel that I am rushing toward my end. My days seem numbered, and it feels that my fate is in cement. Leo waves an AK- 47 around like it's the Mexican flag... Travis snorts his line then takes up a handgun he picked out. I feel like I don't recognize Travis anymore, but that won't stop me from confronting him,

"Travis! Can we talk for a second?" I say.

The mood shifts, and they both look at me like an alien. Travis looks over at Leo for approval then follows me outside. I'm too angry to wait until we're out the door, but I'm walking fast enough for us to already be out of earshot of Leo. I can hear Travis behind me trying to keep up.

"Did you bring me down here to set me up?" I say without turning back.

"What? No. I didn't see this coming, man." He says.

"Angelica told me everything."

"I don't give a fuck what she told you. Don't listen to that crazy bitch." Travis grabs my arm and stops me.

"Why would I kill my best friend?" Travis says.

"Because I know everything. I know about Downtown LA, I know about the drugs, and now I know about your father," I reply. Travis then takes a moment to gather himself and replies, "I'm killing Calderon. We're killing Miguel Calderon. He's the guy that's trying to put us all away." He says.

The look in his eyes is sincere.

"I think I'm going crazy, man," I say.

"One thing I can assure you is that you can't trust a word Angelica says. She's crazy. Okay?" Travis says with a slurred drunken speech.

I submit to end the conversation. I needed time to collect my thoughts.

"Okay," I say. We enter the house, and Leo is waiting for us.

"I found out where he is," Leo says before tossing me a colt.44 magnum.

My heart nearly pounds out of my chest, is this thing loaded? What if I shoot myself? I thought.

"That's the gun you're going to use gringo. Are you ready? Your name is Cortez, why do you look gringo?" Leo says with a smirk.

Travis interjects. "He's half Spanish from Spain."

"It doesn't matter. Have you ever killed anyone," Leo asks?

"That's what we need to talk about." Travis replies,

"What the fuck do we need to talk about?" Leo snaps.

"I'm going to do it," Travis says.

"I can't let you do that. We talked about this." Leo says.

For the first time, I feel like my life is truly in danger and that I heard it with my own ears. I aim the colt.44 at Travis, then at Leo, then back to Travis,

"Talked about what?" I ask. My voice shuddered.

"Dude! Put the gun down! What the fuck are you doing?" Travis asks, terrified.

"No, let him shoot it. He doesn't have the balls. Trust me." Leo says.

I cock the hammer. Travis' eyes widen, and Leo responds quickly, "I promised his dad I would never let him get involved with the murder."

The words infuriate me. "So, you just throw me in front of a gun! Is that it?" I feel like I could pull the trigger.

"It's not like that, bro," Travis says.

"Are you going to shoot or not?"

I aim at Leo, and I'm distracted as he approaches me. He's fearless as somehow, he knows I won't pull the trigger, or does he? Will I? He snatches the gun away and hits me in the head with it. I drop to the ground, dizzy and defeated. He's stronger than he looks, must be the anger I thought. Leo points the gun at me and pulls the trigger several times. It's empty.

"You think I'm going to give you a loaded gun? You stupid motherfucker!"

His boot comes down on my head until I blackout.

XIV.

A blur comes into focus as I wake up and find Angelica standing over me. Was I dead? Wait, I remember Travis bringing me into the bedroom early this morning, but it must've been Angelica who bandaged my sliced wrists? That's the part I have little recollection of. I tried to take my own life, I cracked. How much blood did I lose? Is that why my voice is so raspy? I had so many questions,

"Where is Travis?"

"They already left," She speaks.

"Who? Where?"

"What the fuck were you thinking last night?"

I hold my sore wrist. Blood has stained the white bandages wrapped around them.

"Just answer my question!"

"You know what they want to do." She speaks.

I frantically gather myself and pace around.

"There's nothing you can do about it now. It's done."

I rush for the exit, almost immediately a large guard makes his presence known from the other side of the door. I'm not allowed to leave,

"Get me the fuck out of here!"

Angelica grabs me, "Calm down! If you just shut up, sit down and listen to me, I will help you get out of here!"

Angelica takes my hand, and we move to a back room where she opens a secret door. It takes us outside.

"Follow me."

Leo hands Travis a picture of Calderon as they wait in his truck outside of the bar. Travis is starting to feel fear.

"My guy is expecting you," Leo says.

This is happening and there's no turning back.

"Don't pussy out on me now. After today you're going to be rich and powerful. From a boy to a man. Your days of being a pussy gringo surfer from Malibu are over." Leo tells him.

Travis gets a grip on himself and regains focus. He conceals his pistol and swiftly moves out of the vehicle and into the bar. As he does Calderon rises and moves through the empty cantina and into the bathroom. Beads of sweat have formed on Travis' head. It doesn't deter the bartender from giving him the look of approval. Travis nods back and walks to the bathroom, but before he can enter, Calderon emerges and with his gun drawn shoots him three times. One bullet to the head and two to the chest. Travis drops dead. Before the bartender can react, the DEA agent advances and puts a bullet in his head as he falls over a glass shelf. Leo calmly sits inside of his truck, listening to his radio, oblivious to the hell breaking loose inside the bar. Unaware that he's breathed his last breath until a bullet from

Calderon's gun enters the back of his head. He conceals the weapon and runs away from the scene, away from the sirens approaching in the distance.

XV.

I knew something was wrong as Angelica, and I ran down to Kilometer 38. I knew that because of the helicopters surrounding Leo's hacienda. I had to stay composed because all I knew was that there was no turning back. Angelica hadn't given me all of the information I needed yet, so I had to keep her trust. She was risking her life just like I was, and I had no options.

"They're coming!" She says in a panic.

"Who's coming?"

"La Federales! Shut up and follow me!"

We approach a hidden and inconspicuous trail near the blue water until we reach a cross path.

"This is the only safe place. We have to wait here." She says as gunshots ring out from the Suarez Hacienda.

A whisper in passing is how Angel would learn of the death of Leo, but his heart wouldn't truly be broken until his eyes read the words written in the letter slipped to him. Within seconds he learned of the incestuous relationship his brother and sister indulged in, which served as the motive for why he was set up and put behind bars. One of his trusted assistants, the man, standing behind him, seemed to know exactly how long it would take for him to read and absorb the words. Perhaps a skill he developed watching his boss drink the bad news he had delivered over the years, and when Angel's chin would rise, that was the cue to swipe the blade across his throat. The edge would leave him on the floor to bleed out like an animal with no one to help him. The helicopters abandoned the Suarez Hacienda.

"Okay, listen to me! Follow this path to Cristo del Sagrado Corazon statue. There's a black Jeep parked there. The keys are under the passenger side floor mat."

"What about you?" I ask.

"Don't worry about me. Just listen to what I'm saying. The jeep is legal and will get you back into the states. Angelica begins to run toward the water at Kilometer 38.

"Wait!" I try to stop her. I've developed a genuine interest in her wellbeing.

"Don't wait for me! Let the flowers die!" She turns and doesn't look back.

I want to go after her, but I have to follow her instructions. She walks into the water now and starts to remove her clothes. I run up the hill toward the jeep, knowing I will never see her again. The sun is setting over the deep blue Mexican waters in the pink sky. I notice kids riding around the statue on dirt bikes as I get in the jeep and take the key from under the floor mat, but something comes over me, and I pause, It's calm and peaceful. Despite the chaos around me, I'm compelled to approach the Sagrado Corazon, the statue of Jesus Christ. It reminded me of Zozobra. A giant statue-like effigy that would go up in flames every year back in Santa Fe to cleanse everyone's demons before the annual Fiestas would commence every year. It's like everything around me falls silent as I kneel to say a prayer in my heart. I feel free and unconstrained for the first time since leaving home. I get back in the jeep and start the engine and drive. Angelica vanishes into the blue water, where an apparition of her Mother and an angel appears. Miguel Calderon is in another random bar, and after downing a shot of tequila, he produces his gun and puts a bullet in his head. I don't know if I will see Travis again, but the peace in me says that whatever happened was supposed to happen. I turn on my radio and listen to the news,

"An allegedly high-ranking leader of one of Mexico's largest drug cartels, whose family allegedly heads a faction of the Tijuana drug cartel most powerful drug kingpins, was gunned down today in Mexico. He was ready to face federal narcotics trafficking conspiracy charges in the United States. The defendant, Angel Vicente Suarez, was believed to be one of the most significant Mexican drug defendants that would have been extradited from Mexico to the United States. This result occurred shortly after a local District Attorney was shot at point-blank range in a local Tijuana bar earlier today. The continuing close investigations between the United States and Mexico to prosecute the leaders of international drug trafficking cartels continue."

Retox

I.

The black SUV pulled into the parking lot and parked in front of the Clarity Recovery Rehab Center's main entrance. Palatial views of Zuma beach play in the background of a picturesque ocean manor, laced with palm trees, beautiful flower gardens, and expensive foreign automobiles in the foreground. This was the uber-exclusive beach town of Malibu, California. The driver stepped out and opened the door for the passenger, Cheyanne Mills. It might seem strange for a twenty-seven-year-old woman to be at a place like this, but not in Malibu. It was the norm as that's how this place paid the bills. The price per month to rehabilitate can range from sixty thousand to one hundred and twenty thousand. Still, no amount of money or treatment can make anyone better without an individual's desire to change.

This simple truth was cliché even to those who've never been here. It was due to excessive marketing all over Malibu. It left this rich yet vulnerable population's faith in recovery in the hands of a for-profit business. Keeping people sick with the power of suggestion and perceived diseases diagnosed by well-paid psychiatrists and psychologists is good for business. No one knows this better than the owner and founder of Clarity Recovery, Kurt Roswell. He was the one who had just pulled a shit ton of strings to get Cheyanne from the courtroom to here with a measly five years of probation, which was to start after her treatment here.

The plea bargain entailed a vague summary of the Malibu rehab start-up and nothing else. Cheyanne was a bit confused by the entire thing. The judge's words were still in her head,

"Ms. Mills, your plea is 'guilty' to two counts of third-degree possession with intent to distribute and a count of control."

It was after these words that Cheyanne rolled her eyes. The judge wasn't reading from the papers in front of her and hadn't noticed. Cheyanne wouldn't have cared if she did.

"Now, I see here that you have no criminal record and that you also served your country as a U.S. Marine, so I've decided to mandate you to enter the Clarity Recovery Center's rehab program so that you can get your life together. You got out of jail time by the skin of your teeth, but you will still be sentenced to five years of probation after your rehabilitation is complete. Do you understand?"

Some faces in the courtroom registered a surprising reaction when Cheyanne mumbled the words,

"Yeah, your honor,"

but she got away with it, nevertheless. She didn't understand why Kurt did her this favor, but she really wasn't in any position to reject the gesture, but now it was time for answers. She was greeted as soon as she emerged from the SUV by two sharp women in the forties.

"Hi, I'm Dr. Aubrey Carrington," One said as she extended her hand.

Cheyanne shook it but didn't speak. Perhaps she was intimidated to some degree. Aubrey was a sophisticated and intellectual type. Cheyanne had come from under the table and on the street's kind of life. She was used to stealing and manipulating to obtain her goals. By looking at these two women, she knew that they wouldn't understand her in the back of mind. Not that it was their job to, but to her, these two were the face of this so-called high-profile rehabilitation center, and if everyone here were this uppity, then no one here would understand her.

"Hello Cheyanne, I'm Debbie Levy, "The other woman said, extending the same handshake and smile.

She was more of a corporate type.

"I'm the clinical director here at Clarity," Debbie added.

"I love your name. Do you have Native American Ancestry?" Aubrey asked.

Their charm didn't work on their newest arrival as they were used to.

"I don't mean to be rude, but why did you guys decide to give me the scholarship to come here? Why did that guy Kurt decide to help me? How did he even know me? What's this all about?" Cheyanne demanded.

Debbie cleared her throat, "Cheyanne, we are in the business of helping people. Kurt and the staff here at Clarity want to help people like you recover from addiction. Destiny is what essentially brought you here."

"Where's my cell phone and all of my stuff?"

"You'll get all of your possessions in twenty-four hours. We just have to check you in with one of our nurses and show you to your room. Try and relax. You're in good hands." Debbie said.

"I want to call my sister."

"You can contact her once we get you all checked in," Aubrey said.

II.

Large mahogany panels with luxury furniture, paintings on the walls, and a fancy wooden executive style desk dress Kurt's office. This time of night was peaceful, and this was when he liked reading the DSM-5 while listening to a Bob Proctor meditation on his iPhone. He wore his earbuds but never had the volume too high. He still needed to hear the frequent knocks at his door. This one was from Debbie,

"Cheyanne has been completely processed," She said, standing in the doorway beside Aubrey.

"Yeah, make me sound like I'm a product or something," Cheyanne mumbled.

Debbie couldn't hold back a smirk as she exited and left the two of them alone.

"Have a seat Cheyanne. Can I offer you a drink? The non-alcoholic that is." He laughed, but she didn't.

"Can you tell me why you brought me here?" Cheyenne sighed.

"Cheyanne, you're an addict and a drug dealer." Kurt said.

Her eyes rolled in the same way they did when the judge read her criminal offenses. She knew what she was and didn't take kindly to reminders. Kurt continued.

"The only reason you're not sitting in jail right now is because I don't think you're a bad person. I think you have some underlying issues that can be resolved, which can eventually lead to you living a better life." He said.

"You don't even know me. How did you find me? Why did you find me?" She demanded.

Kurt let out a sigh before responding. "I used to be an addict too. Now, I just want to help people, people like you. That is what we do at Clarity. We try not to do everything solely based on revenue." He explained.

"I'm sorry if I'm a bitch; it's just weird. I mean, I thought I was surely going to do some hard time. I didn't have a lawyer. So, you just sit in courtrooms and try to help people get lighter sentences with rehab?" She asked.

"Not necessarily. We're a little more selective than that. Most of the time, I'm looking for people that have not yet reached the point of no return. Meaning they can still save themselves,"

Kurt said.

"Well, I don't know if I'm the right candidate, man. I'm jonesing right now." Cheyanne said.

"Withdrawals are brutal, I know. How did you manage in jail?" He asked.

"I already had a prescription for suboxone, so they let me take it after the second week. The first week was hell." She explained.

"We treat clients with something ugh more effective than suboxone here. It's called 'KISS' similar to that of suboxone, but much fewer side effects,"

Kurt opened his desk drawer and produced a medicine bottle of pills and handed it to Cheyanne.

"Here, this is for you. Take one in the morning and once at night. It will help. Trust me." He said with a smile.

She took the bottle, somewhat confused, "Shouldn't a nurse be giving me this stuff?"

"The sooner, the better," Kurt said as he handed her a bottle of water.

"Get some rest tonight, tomorrow we'll go to the Four Seasons spa. Think of it as a detox orientation," He gave her a wink.

"Well, I'm not going to say no to that," Cheyanne said as she finally let a slight smile escape her hardened features.

"You're in good hands, Cheyanne."

Cheyanne was still a bit foggy from the drugs Kurt gave her. He woke her up around noon. That wasn't the strangest part; however, it was the fact that he came into her room. She held in her anger when she learned that her blurred senses were an average side effect of the medication that would last for the first few days of taking it. He should've warned her, is what she thought. There was no telling of when she'd remember that she forgot her phone. Too much was happening around her, to see through this cloud. She tried to call her sister last night but got her voicemail. Her mind was somewhere else now, with her eyes fixed on the facade of the beautiful Ritz Carlton hotel.

"Come on; we're going to have some fun," Kurt said as he shifted into park.

He got out first and opened Cheyanne's door. She was obviously out of her element as she stepped out of Kurt's red Ferrari Enzo. Cheyanne was borderline catatonic at this point. Kurt immediately made himself at home in the uber lavish suite, almost like it was routine. The room had everything you'd expect and more.

"Is this a wonderful place or what?" He asked.

"Yeah, I guess. Where is the spa?" She asked.

"Let's relax a little first. There's no rush," Kurt said calmly.

He reached into the mini bar, then opened a half bottle of wine and poured into two glasses. Cheyanne was shocked at the sight, "What are you doing? I thought you were a doctor or whatever. You're giving me booze?"

"Booze?" He corrected her. "Wine is good for us." Kurt said.

"Are you high?"

"Yes," Kurt replied with a smile.

"Are you on heroin?" She asked, then tried to make her way to the exit.

"Where are you going?" Kurt pulled a hypodermic needle, cotton balls, spoon, and tie-off out of his leather bag.

Cheyanne stopped in her tracks. She couldn't help herself and turn back from exiting. Her eyes focused on the lighter as it melted the Heroin into liquid,

"What are you trying to do to me?" She asked.

"It's either this or jail." He said sternly.

III.

Echo Mills was Cheyanne's sister, who was older by two years. She was a natural brunette beauty, thin and elegant in a biker bitch kind of way. She thought she was up to date on her sister's whereabouts, but she too had accidentally left her phone at her previous location, a Texas automotive garage. That's why she had missed her sister's calls and texts and hadn't been in the loop. The street life was a fast one, and her baby sister only knew how to navigate because of her. Echo taught Cheyanne everything she knew, even how to forget a phone. What you wouldn't know by looking at her is that at this Texas automotive garage was a scene of carnage left by Echo and the friend she had with her, Lonnie Rossi. She was tattooed, blonde and sexy in a biker bitch kind of way, fully capable of taking a dick. They tried to sell the motorcycle they've been riding to some Mexicans, and the deal went south. Not for Echo and Lonnie, though. Two beautiful white girls like themselves would be naive to initiate such a transaction without being prepared for the worst. When the Mexicans tried to take the thirty grand they initially offered and the bike, that's when the girls drew their guns, and before it was all said and done, the conmen were trapped in a gasoline lit ring of fire that nearly burned down the garage. The girls took off with the money and the bike, and now they were filling up the tank. They justify the goods they obtain because they only take what they take from rapists and murderers. This motorcycle was a pristine and glistening nineteen fifty-two Harley Davidson Panhead chopper that belonged to a pig of a man named Ghost. He had grabbed Echo's ass in a bar the night before, and she kept her calm and accepted his challenge, which was a game of pool where the stakes were a blow job back at his place. If she won, it was a hundred-dollar bill, and Ghost would pay the tab. Her and Lonnie already had the scoop on this guy, which is why the Echo let him beat her in the pool. He was a rapist, so they showed no mercy when he took them back to his place. He received an ass- kicking, and they received a new bike. Echo rode this one, and Lonnie rode the Harley Davidson FXR.

"Shit, Cheyanne texted last night." Lonnie said as she searched her phone.

"What? I thought she was in L.A. County," Echo said.

"Well, the text says nine one one," Lonnie said.

"Where the fuck is, she?" Echo asked.

"Rehab in Malibu."

Echo looked at the texts on Lonnie's phone.

"What the fuck did she get herself involved in now? I knew she was chasing the dragon again,"

Echo said as she shook her head,

"Well, let's gas up and head to Cali," Lonnie said.

"Time to go and bail out lil sis again."

Kurt had stepped out of the shower and wrapped a large towel around his waist. At the same time, he took a large swig from a vodka bottle and entered the bedroom area. It's apparent that he and Cheyanne have just had sex and were in the intermission of a drug-filled marathon. Cheyanne was lying on the bed, half-naked and visibly high. She reached for the counter to grab another needle and tie-off to shoot up again.

"Stop!" Kurt shouted, "We have to sober up and get back to Clarity. Remember, don't let the drug control you; you control the drug," He added.

This was his shady motto for whatever partner he could find to shoot up with. Only an addict would believe such words.

"I'm just going to take more," Cheyanne said softly.

"Okay. Screw it; I will too," Kurt sat beside her on the bed and lit up the spoon while she tied up her arm. The needle punctured her vein, and she sat still in a euphoric state. Kurt went and finished the rest of the vodka, then returned to the bed and prepared a needle for himself. After injecting the Heroin, he stood from the ground and removed his towel before turning on music. Completely naked, he began dancing around the room. Cheyanne didn't notice at first when he abruptly slowed down and dropped to the floor. It wasn't until moments after he was passed out that she saw him. That's when she rushed over to try and wake him to no avail.

"Kurt! Kurt! Wake up!" She screamed.

When she realized this wouldn't work, she filled a bucket with ice and water to splash on his face, but he remained unconscious. She desperately called the front desk. It was the last thing she wanted to do. What would happen to her and Kurt? He had been the reason that she relapsed.

"I have an emergency in my room! He's unconscious! There's a man in my room that's not breathing!" She screamed.

IV.

Large semi-trucks in full swing Peterbilt's, Mack's, Kenworth's, are all parked in the lot of a truck stop where American drivers slept, drank coffee, called their wives, and ate gas station hot dogs. Echo and Lonnie pulled up and parked their bikes. They found a stash spot along the property's perimeter and buried the money they got from the Mexicans at the automotive garage. They produced their needles and began to shoot up Heroin. Three Mexican women in their forties, who were probably the truckers' girlfriends, entered and headed toward the ladies' room. They were visibly intoxicated. Echo and Lonnie walked in behind them. The women were lining up cocaine along with a makeup mirror on top of the counter near the sinks. They were loud and obnoxious as they spoke in Spanish. They were probably talking badly about Echo and Lonnie. The two of them went on about their business until one of the Mexican women snapped a picture of Lonnie's chaps with a cell phone.

"What the fuck are you doing?" Lonnie shouted.

"I've never seen pants like that. Do you shake your ass in those pants?" The woman asked.

"Fuck you, cunt!" Lonnie replied. She got on the woman's face. One of the other women pulled out a knife,

"You want to fuck around bitch?" The knife-wielding woman shouted.

Echo stepped in between them, "Take it easy. What's your problem?" Echo asked.

"We don't like the way you look," One of the women replied.

Echo head-butted the woman, and the knife fell to the ground. Lonnie picked it up, then quickly moved behind one of the other women and held the knife to her neck,

"You looking for a knife fight?" Lonnie said in the woman's ear.

The women spoke something submissive in Spanish, "Lo Siento. Por Favor."

Lonnie let the woman go before shoving her against a wall. All three women have defeated themselves. They tried to stay standing, leaning up against the bathroom walls. They looked a mess and Echo and Lonnie made their exit with angry eyes fixed on the three women.

"Just say no to drugs," Echo said before putting the woman's knife in her pocket.

They didn't contest their silverware being taken; Lonnie laughed. As they stepped outside, they were greeted by Ghost, Jumbo, and Tito,

"Hi girls!" Ghost said with a smile.

Tito had a gun and the passenger door open to the black Bronco.

"Give me back my gun and get your asses in the back of the car," Jumbo said.

Ghost drove with Tito in the passenger seat, with his gun pointed at Echo and Lonnie as they sat in the backseat next to Jumbo,

"You gals fucked up. You know that, right? Where the fuck is the bike?" Jumbo demanded.

"Fuck, all three of you." Echo said.

"You know it's funny, all this time you've been selling me stolen bikes that belonged to rapists and killers, but little did you know that you were selling those bikes to a rapist and a killer. Tonight, you are going to find out first-hand what rape and murder are all about," Jumbo said.

Lonnie slowly slipped out the knife she took from the Mexican woman and placed a firm grip on the handle. She swiftly stabbed Tito in the neck and brought back the gun, Blood was everywhere. Echo started punching Jumbo as hard as she could while Ghost ignored the road and lost control of the vehicle. The Bronco spun and landed in an embankment as Tito cried as he bled out,

"No, Sobrevivir. No, Sobrevivir!"

Echo and Lonnie crawled out. No back windows. The Ghost was in bad shape after having bashed his head against the windshield. Echo dragged him out and pushed him to the ground,

"Let's kill these assholes once and for all," Lonnie said.

"No, we don't kill. We have rules, remember?" Echo said.

Lonnie had the gun drawn on Jumbo and forced him out of the Bronco as well. He didn't have a leg to stand on. Echo and Lonnie got in and drove off, leaving the thugs stranded.

V.

Cheyanne has had a long night. She sat in a nurse's office, waiting for medication. An Asian nurse had been logging her information,

"Did you eat breakfast yet?" The nurse asked her.

"I'm not hungry; where is my cell phone?" Cheyanne snapped back.

"I'm not sure. You shouldn't take any medication on an empty stomach."

Cheyanne rolled her eyes. "Is there something like lost and found here? I need my phone."

The nurse handed Cheyanne a couple of tables and a small cup of water.

"Regarding the medication, check back in with me in a couple of hours," The nurse said calmly.

"That's it? You're like a modern-day Florence Nightingale." Cheyanne said. She downed the pills and walked out.

As soon as she stepped out of the nurse's office, she was approached by Dr. Carrington,

"Cheyanne! We still have a few minutes before the group. Can I speak to you in my office for a minute?"

"Do I have a choice?" Cheyanne said as she followed Dr. Carrington into her office. She entered to see Debbie waiting for her. "Hello, Cheyanne," She said with a smile.

"Go ahead and grab a seat, Cheyanne." Dr. Carrington said as she sat at her desk.

"So, Cheyanne, it came to my attention that you had a strange ordeal occur last night. You relapsed. Is this true?" Debbie asked.

Cheyanne looked at Debbie, "Are you fucking serious?"

"Answer the question," Debbie said.

She turned back to Dr. Carrington.

"I fucking relapsed because of the owner or whatever the fuck he is of this place gave it to me," Cheyanne said. Dr. Carrington cleared her throat,

"We're talking about you right now, Cheyanne. No one is judging you. I think both Kurt and Debbie made it very clear to you where we stand with discretion. Kurt's situation and your situation are two separate accounts. I'm trying to help you understand that relapse is part of recovery. It's progress." Dr. Carrington said.

"Progress?" Cheyanne was angry now.

Dr. Carrington saw this and turned to Debbie.

"Deb, can you give us a moment alone?" Debbie quietly removed herself from the room.

"Cheyanne, the reason Kurt did what he did last night was to help you. We're going the distance here, man, trying to cover everyone's perspective. Maybe last night was all just a test?" Dr. Carrington suggested.

"That's a bunch of bullshit, Kurt was trying to get me high so he could fuck me! As soon as his plan backfired and almost overdosed, for god's sake, he and Debbie then decided to blackmail me by threatening to set me up if I say anything. Now you are trying to manipulate me. This is all bullshit." Cheyanne said.

"Cheyanne, you're having irrational thoughts right now. You're paranoid."

"Give me a fucking break. I just want to get the fuck out of this place." Cheyanne replied.

"I hate to break it to you, but it's either this or jail." Dr. Carrington said calmly.

"Great, then take me back to jail, please."

Dr. Carrington sighed, "It's not that easy, kiddo. I want you to take a moment and breathe. Relax. I'm not attacking you; I want you and every other client here, including myself, to start getting in the habit of holding ourselves accountable for both the good and the terrible things we do in this life."

"You should give this speech to Kurt. If anyone needs to hold themselves accountable, it's him."

"You're worrying about other people besides yourself again," Dr. Carrington said.

"Maybe because what he did affected me and pushed me back into relapsing," Cheyanne replied.

"Now you're making excuses," Dr. Carrington said sternly.

Cheyanne moves toward the door,

"I'm done for now. I have to go to this group thing, I guess."

"You can learn to reframe your thoughts! You are free to reframe any thought you ever have into something more positive! Are you aware of this?" Dr. Carrington asked.

"Listen, I still have a headache from last night. Can we finish this later?"

"Usually, I'm the one that ends the conversation, but given our circumstances, you are dismissed from the group. I would like to have another session with you tomorrow. By the way, 'Love is the Final Answer' group is ground-breaking and one of the best groups in the industry," Dr. Carrington said.

"What is that?" Cheyanne asked.

"It's the group you're going to right now," Dr. Carrington replied.

"Do I have to go," Cheyanne asked? Dr. Carrington just smiled. Cheyanne knew the answer was yes.

VI.

Clients entered the room, and on their way to their seats, they passed the chalkboard where 'Love is the Final Answer' was written in large letters. Cheyanne was one of the last to enter, but not the last. That title would go to Kurt, who entered incognito wearing sunglasses as the doors were shut behind him. Cheyanne sat uncomfortably before the group began to clap for Kurt, who stood before the room to speak,

"It ain't easy, this path that we're all on is not easy. We have to take deep, long, and intense looks down deep into ourselves. Our flaws, our past, our sins, everything. We look at these things, and we feel something guilt, anger, depression, to name a few. Do these things define us? Are we wrong? Are we bad people? How did we end up here? These are all the questions we may, or may not, ask ourselves," Kurt sighs deeply as if a weight has been lifted off of him.

Some faces in the room register with intrigue. Cheyanne's is one of the faces that registers a disconnect and lack of interest. Kurt continued,

"There will be no interaction today, I will not ask any of your personal questions. We will not try to demystify anything. We are simply going to sit here and 'Be.' Just sit here with me in silence and, 'Be,'" He said.

The room remained silent as Kurt took his seat. He closed his eyes as if he were practicing some sort of medication. Cheyanne watched as some of the uncomfortable audience members eventually adapted and began to do the same. At no point during the meeting did she adapt like the others. Cheyanne and a few other clients walked out of the room after the meeting and noticed that a new client was being checked into the facility. More specifically, what caught Cheyanne's eye was that a nurse escorted the new client to the room next to hers. He was tall, slim, and handsome and she overheard his name being said by the nurse. "Trace Andreen", she heard it because it's what she wanted to hear. Cheyanne had begun to walk back toward her room when Kurt intercepted her,

"Can I talk to you?" He said, keeping his voice low.

"Can I just go to my room?" Cheyanne asked.

"I just want to apologize for what happened at the Four Seasons. We are all very vulnerable. I just had to go through what I went through; it's part of the process," He said calmly.

"At the expense of other people?" Cheyanne replied.

"I know that you are going to get better here. You just have to receive what we are giving you. Even what happened at the hotel it was a gift. It gave you a perspective at my expense. You see, it's all relative. It's all about receiving and being grateful," Kurt said.

Trace's father emerged from his room and waved at Kurt from down the hall, "Mr. Roswell, can I bend your ear for a sec?"

"Hey Steve, call me Kurt. Of course, I'm here for you and your son! He's already looking better. I don't want you to worry about a thing. We heal people here!" Kurt said with a smile as he shifted into a corporate mode to shake Steve's hand.

He nodded at Cheyanne. Trace emerged from his room and approached her, "Do you have a cigarette?" He asked.

"No, but I need one too. Let's go outside."

He followed her out and watched her bum a couple of smokes from a random client.

"I don't even smoke, but now seems like a perfect time to start. What's your name?" She asked.

"Trace. What's yours?"

"Cheyanne. I know it's one of those hippy-dippy names."

"I like it." Trace said with a smile.

She smiled back, "What are you in for?" She asked.

"Drugs."

"Duh. I know that. What kind of drugs?"

"Heroin." Trace said.

"The white lady got you too, huh?" Cheyanne said as she exhaled.

"Yeah, I'm still alive, though. I guess," Trace shrugged then continued. "Detox is so brutal. I feel like shit."

"What kind of meds did they give you? I don't even know, to be honest. I just took whatever they gave me," He said.

Cheyanne gave Trace and his father a moment to say their goodbyes. She finished her cigarette alone.

"Son, you got this," Steve said then continued, "You're in good hands here. Be strong and do what they tell you. I love you, son."

"I'm going to try hard this time, papa. I'm tired of letting you down," Trace said.

"You're never going to let me down, Trace. I love you, no matter what. You're my son," They hugged.

Kurt jogged out to send Steve off, "He's safe with us! We're going to win this battle!" Kurt reassured Steve.

Trace walked back over to Cheyanne to finish his cigarette and Kurt's eyes followed. He didn't like the bonding that he witnessed taking place between Cheyanne and Trace. He intervened,

"Trace, do you mind if I speak to Cheyanne alone?" Kurt asked.

Trace put out the cigarette and walked back inside.

"Do you like him?"

"What? What are you talking about?" She asked.

"Are you attracted to Trace? It's a simple question."

"No. Why would you ask that question? Why would it be any of your business?" She asked.

"I just want to make one thing clear to you right now, there are no carnal relations between clients in the house," He said.

"What about carnal relations between you and your clients?" She asked.

"Excuse me?" Kurt said.

"Is it okay for you to exploit my addiction by giving me drugs and trying to fuck me?" Cheyanne demanded.

Kurt discreetly lit a cigarette, "That kind of talk will get you nowhere," He said.

"By the way, my cell phone just vanished all of a sudden. I don't even know how to contact my family. All of my numbers are in my phone."

"Don't worry, we'll find it must be here somewhere. You probably just left it somewhere," Kurt said.

"Yeah, I must've been under the influence of some strange drug, right? By the way, what was the name of that stuff you guys have been giving me? I need more," She said.

"We have to monitor your intake we don't just hand out medication like candy here. I should tell you this now, be careful around our new client, Trace. He suffers from an extreme addiction to Heroin he's in Detox right now, so maybe it's better if you just try to avoid him for a couple of days," Kurt said.

"We just met. I'm trying to avoid everyone here can you get me high, please?" Kurt became paranoid, "No, not today. There are people around." Kurt rushed off.

VII.

Cheyanne was in a towel fresh out of the shower when someone knocked on her door. Before she could answer it, the door creaked open slowly it was Trace who, at this point, was restless and seeking company,

"Can I come in, please? It's an emergency."

She secretly allowed him in, "We could get into a lot of trouble being in this room together. Let me get dressed, and we'll smoke outside."

"Okay, but hurry, please. I have so much anxiety right now. This place is freaking me out," Trace said.

"Hang in there, okay, meet me downstairs in the courtyard," Cheyanne said before she shut the door behind him and swiftly dressed.

Her words failed to ease his nerves as Trace paced back and forth in the courtyard as he waited for her. She approached him with a pack of cigarettes,

"Are you alright?" She asked.

"I gotta get the fuck out of this place, man. My friend, Kyle, is coming to get me."

"You mean they released you?" Cheyanne asked, surprised.

"No, I'm just going to leave, plus, he's bringing some drugs. You should come with us," Trace suggested.

"I can't." She said.

"Why not?"

"If I leave this place, I'm going to jail."

"Jail? For what?" Trace asked.

"It's a long story Kurt is blackmailing me. He tried to sleep with me the other night. Please don't tell anyone," She said.

"Are you serious? This is so fucked up I knew there was something shady about this place," Trace said.

"I can't even get in touch with my sister because he took my phone. I don't know what to do."

Trace didn't hesitate to pull out his phone,

"Here Call her!"

"I don't have my number memorized. See, I'm fucked," Cheyanne sighed.

"Just come with us, and we'll figure everything out later. Don't worry, we'll find her," Trace said.

"Fuck. Okay, let me get my stuff," Cheyanne said.

"Hurry and do that, and I'll go up to the main road near the gate to meet Kyle. We're going to be in a white Jeep waiting for you!"

"Okay!" Cheyanne shouted over her shoulder as she ran inside.

She tactfully rushed to her room to grab her things. Once she was inside, she dropped the facade and frantically began to grab her clothing along with shoes and makeup items, placing her stuff in bags then putting on her jacket. Kurt abruptly walked in,

"Going somewhere?" He asked.

"No."

"You're going to meet Trace and his friend, right?"

"No, I'm just trying to clean my room," She said.

It was the fact that she was holding all of her things and wearing a jacket that made it hard for Kurt to believe her. They both seemed to realize this before Cheyanne dropped her bags. A tall, tattooed, cholo like R.A. (resident assistant/tech) stood in Trace's room and kept an intimidating eye on him while he sat anxiously on his bed, holding an unlit cigarette.

"Cortez, can I at least go outside and smoke this cigarette? You can come with me."

"Nope," Cortez said.

"This is fucking bullshit, man. I want my phone; I have to call my dad. Give me my phone, please."

"I don't have your phone. Listen, I'm just doing my job. You can't leave this room until Kurt gets here."

"He's such a pussy. What does he hire a bunch of gang members with tattoos to do his dirty work? He can't face me like a grown-up?" Trace asked.

"You tried to sneak out of here, and you got caught. Why are you blaming everyone else? We're trying to help you. By the way, I'm not a gangster either, just because I'm Mexican with tattoos doesn't necessarily make me a gang member," Cortez said.

"I'm sorry, man. I'm just so pissed off right now," Trace said.

"It's fine. As I said, I'm just doing my job. You don't think I want to be at home with my wife and kids?"

Trace was surprised, "You have a wife and kids?"

"What? Gangsters can't have a family?"

Path stood to shake Cortez's hand, "I apologize I didn't mean to profile you like that."

Cortez shrugged, "All good, man I'm brown, with ink, and I'm wearing a Dodgers hat because I'm a true fan of the team, and I'm from L.A.," Cortez said.

Trace sat back down and began to fidget with stuff. His nervousness escalated Cortez took note of it and sympathized with him,

"Go ahead and smoke, but just blow it out the window."

Trace jumped at the opportunity and lit up the cigarette.

"How do you like it out here in L.A.?" Trace asked.

"You mean Malibu?"

"Malibu is L.A.," Trace said.

"No, it's not, where I live is Los Angeles. Malibu is not L.A.," Cortez said sternly.

"What part of L.A. do you live in?" Trace asked.

"Downtown near Olvera Street. As real as it gets."

"So, it's pretty dangerous?"

"No, man you watch way too many movies. Olvera Street is the birthplace of L.A it's in the heart of Los Angeles with a marketplace and amazing Mexican restaurants," Cortez explained.

"I love Mexican food," Trace said.

"Who doesn't?" Cortez asked. Their attention was taken away by a knock at the door. It was Kurt who entered like the room was his own,

"There's no smoking allowed in the house, Trace," Kurt said as he nodded to Cortez.

This was his signal to leave them alone.

"You can wait outside, please. Thank you."

Cortez stepped outside and closed the door.

"So, what were you thinking, Trace? You haven't even been here for twenty-four hours."

"This place just isn't for me, man. I'm jonesin like crazy."

"Your father would be very disappointed if he found out about this."

"Please don't tell him, I just need more meds to get through this," Trace begged.

"I know you were planning to take Cheyanne with you," Kurt said.

"What do you mean?" Trace asked.

"Please don't insult my intelligence, listen to me very carefully; stay away from her," Kurt said.

He took away Trace's cigarette, put it out on the windowsill,

"Lights out. Get to bed," Kurt said over his shoulder as he left the room.

VIII.

Cheyanne slept as light entered from the crack in the door. It was Trace who quietly eased into her room and admired her angelic glance for a moment before she awoke. She was startled by the silhouetted figure at the foot of her bed, but she calmed her senses upon realizing it was Trace,

"What are you doing here?"

"I have a present for you," Trace said.

"What?"

Trace produced a bag of Heroin and a needle from his pant pocket.

"How did you get it in?" She asked.

"When I'm desperately in need, I'll find away,"

Trace said with a smile she puckered up out of bed, and it wasn't long before they were shooting up under the moonlight. The intravenous needle was injected into her vein. Trace smoked it chased the dragon. Both were high and feeling the euphoric sensation of the drug together, and everything faded away. An intimacy overtook both of them, and they made love. A roadside bar reminiscent of the Double Deuce lit up the open road and resounds Roadhouse sameness as the Blues were heard from afar. Echo and Lonnie pulled up and parked near the bar entrance to drink a beer and rest after a long day of riding. Inside were wood panel walls, red vinyl booths, and an old antique bar with cushioned armrests. A stripper pole loomed in the center of the room and the place was empty except for the two men who sat at the bar. One was tall, big, and covered with tattoos that was

Tank. The other was Elmer, the bartender. His build was the opposite of Tanks. Thin and short with a pot marked face from a life of drug use. Tank finished chugging a PBR and chased it with a shot of tequila from the bottle sitting on the bar. He poured it himself.

"I know this is blasphemy, but I always thought PBR tastes like piss water. Schlitz, now that's a good tasting beer," Tank said.

"Pabst Blue Ribbon owns Schlitz! If it's American, I'll drink it, but some of the Mexican beers are good too. Pacifico with a lime. That's a good one," Elmer replied.

"I once saw a donkey show in Mexico. Great whores and good tequila, but I'll pass on the beer," Tank said.

"To each his own," Elmer replied.

They noticed the girls enter.

"Welcome, ladies! What can we pour you?" Elmer asked.

"Two Pacifico's, please," Echo said.

"With limes, please," Lonnie added.

"Excellent choice!" Elmer said as the girls sat at the bar to rest a bit.

"Where are you ladies from?" Tank asked.

"Texas," Echo replied.

"What ya'll do in Mexico?" Tank asked.

"Riding through," Echo said.

"You gals better be careful on motorcycles. My nephew killed himself on one of the things," Elmer said.

"They're dangerous, but then again, so are a lot of things in this world, right?" Echo asked.

"I reckon so," Elmer answered.

Tank jumped in. "So, you two must like to live on the edge."

"No, we are just regular girls that like beer and motorcycles. By the way, why is there a stripper pole in here?" Echo asked.

"Tell her, Elmer," Tank said.

"Well, have you ever seen that movie, Showgirls? Well, let's just say that movie changed my life forever!"

"I think you may be watching too many movies, Elmer," Echo said.

"What about your friend? Is she a mute? "Asked Tank.

"Only to Chachi's like you," Said Lonnie.

"Echo and Lonnie grab their beers before heading to a table.

"A couple of females, badass types. I know women like that Y'all ain't the type that thinks you're equal to men, are you?" Tank asked as he downed another tequila shot.

"Look, man, we just want to drink our beers and relax. We're not trying to start any trouble," Echo said.

Tank took another shot then slammed the empty glass on the table.

"And just like that, you two Texas cunts come into my bar to start some shit, thinking you're better than everyone. Well, let me tell you something, my bar, my rules," Tank said before he pulled out a gun.

Elmer moved and locked the front door and shut off the 'open' light as if on cue.

"Y'all are gonna dance for us tonight," Tank said with a smile.

He moved closer to the women with the gun aimed at them, then continued,

"Take your clothes off and dance."

"You're kidding, right?" Echo asked.

Tank cocked the gun,

"Elmer! Turn on some music and grab the handcuffs."

Elmer followed orders. Buck Owens', 'Cryin Time,' played on the jukebox. Tank began dancing and waving the gun around as he moved closer and closer to the women. Lonnie suddenly launched her glass, half full, full speed at Tank's head. It stunned him, and the women both leaped up and bum-rushed him. At this point, Elmer knew he was in trouble. He ran behind the bar and watched as Lonnie took Tank's gun while Echo held him down.

"Who's the cunt now, pervert?" Echo demanded.

"Please don't kill me! Please, I have kids!" Tank begged.

Lonnie walked behind the bar and found Elmer, who cried with fear. She shook her head at sight.

"Why are pervert rapists all such pathetic cowards?" She asked Echo.

"Because they don't have balls," Lonnie broke open the bar register and took all of the money then stuffed it in her purse. Echo held the gun to Tank's head.

"Grow some balls bitch," Echo said.

Lonnie used the handcuffs to tie Tank and Elmer's hands together around the stripper pole. The dolls calmly made their exit and got on their motorcycles. They rode past the sign that read, 'Welcome to Mexico. The Land of Enchantment'.

IX.

A nurse patiently knocked on the door a few times but didn't get an answer. That's when she decided to let herself in, and that's when she saw Cheyanne and Trace still in bed and in no hurry to wake up. It's obvious to her that the two of them slept together. She saw the drug paraphernalia on the small table beside them. She did nothing now but returned with Debbie and Cortez, who were both in complete shock. Cortez quickly rushed in to wake the two of them. A massive, antique chandelier hung above the glass conference table where Debbie, Cortez, Dr. Carrington, a nurse, and therapist sat in anticipation of an overdue meeting.

The twenty-nine-year-old therapist was an educated and sophisticated Hispanic woman. Angelica. She was the first to notice Kurt walk in.

"So, I hear we had a situation last night," Kurt said.

"A situation. Cheyanne and Trace were caught in the act of sexual copulation. They were also using," Debbie said.

Kurt was abnormally calm, "How did they get the drugs?" He asked Cortez.

"The guy that drove here to pick up Trace when he was trying to discharge must have slipped him something before, we caught him out there," Cortez explained.

"Where are they now?" Kurt asked.

"Cheyanne is passed out in her room, and Trace is in detox with a nurse right now," Debbie said.

"Trace is still here?" Angelica asked.

"Where else would he be?" Kurt asked.

"Shouldn't he be discharged for breaking the rules? I mean, he could have hurt someone, and he took advantage of a client under the influence. He's dangerous," Angelica vented.

"I understand your concern and frustration, but we can't just abandon our clients," Said Kurt.

"It's also our moral obligation to protect our clients," Angelica replied.

"May I remind you that I'm the clinical director, owner of this facility. Don't ever question my authority," Kurt said. He continued, "You can leave."

Angelica was dumbfounded as she made her exit. Kurt closed the door behind her.

"As far as the situation last night, It never happened," Kurt said.

Everyone looked around confused. "This meeting is dismissed," Kurt added.

Everyone made their exit except for Dr. Carrington, "Do you think you were a little harsh on our little miss ethical little therapist?" She asked Kurt.

"To be frank, I'm tired of her attitude. She's always trying to act as if she's in charge of something and she's probably one of those female empowerment fanatics," He said.

"It's just a defense mechanism don't give her that much power. You're wasting energy."

"I feel like shit, man, I didn't get any sleep last night, and I'm on edge," Kurt said.

"You need to cool on the partying, mate take a couple of days off," She said.

"I can't believe that cunt was trying to run my meeting."

"Trace's father called a bit ago. Said Dr. Carrington.

"Does he know what happened last night?" Kurt asked.

"Oh, god no, he just called to make sure we got the check. Debbie just made all the deposits, so we're good," Dr. Carrington said.

"Do you see what I mean? We have to look at things from a fiscal perspective, I kick out a Trace on account of some ethical nonsense, and we lose a hundred grand. Am I doing the right thing, doc?" Kurt asked.

"We're just selling dreams here, Kurt. This facility is just a resort for people to drop off their junkie kids or crazy fathers and mothers so they can get a time out for a month." She continued, "Sure, we can provide the therapy and meds, but in the end, the client has to want to get clean to stay clean, we're just running a business." Dr. Carrington said.

"Kiss is our real ticket out of the middle. I mean, yeah, we turned a five-million-dollar investment into ten million in three years, but I think Kiss is going to be the real breadwinner!" He said.

"Agreed, we just have to make sure that 'Kiss' is officially classified as a 'benzo' when given to clients. You and I can call it whatever we want, but the FDA and DEA surely would not appreciate us creating our drug without them knowing. We have to be very careful about this. only you and I are to know this. Kurt! I'm fucking serious. Only you and I."

"Ten-four, Doctor, can you just tell me what the fuck is actually in it?" Asked Kurt.

"Long story short, it's just Fentanyl laced with high octane heroin. It keeps addicts wanting more but also acts kind of like suboxone. This way, the client may be in Detox here at Clarity. Still, they are actually in addiction purgatory which keeps them coming back. This way, when they check out of here and go back out in the real world, they can be susceptible to relapse, and then they can check back in here, and we can charge them again, and it becomes one big fucking vicious cycle. Yes, we are a couple of evil fucks that found a hole in the system and are cashing in on it."

"We're fucking bad, I mean fucked." Kurt said.

Dr. Carrington broke out a line of cocaine on a makeup mirror.

"It's fucking American capitalism, American dream whatever the fuck! It's just business. I'm not Doctor Phil, and you certainly are not. It's even worse than it appears we're just a holding station. The war on drugs is much more complicated and there are so many layers. As I said, we're just selling dreams," She said.

Kurt attacked a line of cocaine. "By the way, I've got the heroin we confiscated from Trace." She said. They both indulged "Fuck, I've got to get ready to be on T.V.," Kurt said.

X.

The dolls pulled up to what looked like a sort of hippie commune. Psychedelic sculptures, glass bottle mosaics, and Tibetan wind flags were in abundance. A man named Zen walked out from the back and he smoked a joint and carried a portable Bluetooth speaker playing Native American flute music. Marijuana farming was in full swing in the green room. This explained his relaxed demeanor.

"Welcome to the arm!" He said to Echo and Lonnie.

An Italian bodybuilder waited inside to greet the girls. Zen directed the girl's attention toward him, "By the way, this is Tony."

"Welcome," Tony said with a smile.

"Jerry! Seriously? This is a beautiful place," Echo said.

"My name is Zen now, don't worry; it's cool It's been way too long, Echo! I'm glad you guys haven't killed yourselves on those motorcycles yet. The last time I saw you and Cheyanne was like ten years ago. How is she, by the way?"

"She's not doing too well; we are actually on our way to L.A. to get her. She's got a drug problem, and apparently, she's at some sketch rehab out there," Echo said.

"How did she end up in L.A," Zen asked.

"Your guess is as good as mine," Echo said.

"Drugs? What kind of drugs?"

"Heroin, What else?" Echo said.

"Aw, the devil's drug. That drug is evil, man. People all dropping like flies from that shit all over the world. I had a dance with that stuff and soon realized the extent of its wickedness. If you're going to do a drug, Mary Jane is the real cure," Zen said. He continued, "Come inside let me show you around. We have three hundred square feet of marijuana plants in the growing process."

"What the fuck!" Lonnie said.

"Growing up in Montecito, man all the people I knew were rich kids that are dead now from drugs. Drugs like Heroin and meth to be exact," Zen said.

"Wait, weren't we the ones selling them the drugs?" As asked before, they both started laughing.

"We did make a lot of money, hundreds of thousands of dollars, but it was time to get the fuck out of that place. Those days are all behind me now, I'm not Jerry Rubinstein anymore. Meet the new me all Zen! Now I'm on a raw diet, hemp advocate, and grower, Landowner. I spend most of my time with my dogs, man. We have ayahuasca tea parties here, Fucking Ram Dass readings, intense meditation sessions. We even go crystal hunting! I fucking love my life."

"How long have you been out here doing this?" Echo asked.

"About six years now, I love it! Fresh air, blue skies, amazing sunsets. We're just waiting for the New Mexico State legislature to legalize. We have locations all over the state, ready to open. In the meantime, we're supplying Colorado and Cali. There's a lot of money and opportunity in this industry. It's growing every day," Zen said.

"Yeah, but it's technically still illegal in this state to even grow, right?" Echo asked.

"Yes, but we're hoping they legalize soon," Zen said.

They went inside for a tour, and the girls went straight upstairs to the ladies' room. It was only a few moments later that they overheard two sheriffs knock down the front door and scream,

"Sheriff's department! Get the fuck down! Put your hands up and get down on the floor now!"

The gunshots that followed made the girls freeze, but Lonnie managed to move into a position to peek over the ledge where she saw Zen and Tony shot dead.

"They fucking killed Zen and Tony. They're not sheriffs. This is a heist," She said just loud enough for Echo to hear.

"We gotta get the fuck out of here right now," Lonnie said.

"How?" Echo asked.

They both move to a window and examine the twenty-foot drop. "We've jumped further down than that, haven't we?" Echo asked.

"I'm not sure, but we don't have a choice."

They hop on the window ledge and get ready to jump for the long fall.

"Just land on your feet and make sure to bend your knees," Lonnie said.

They both jumped and grabbed onto a plank on the way down to absorb some of the impact. They quickly got on their bikes and hauled ass while taking gunfire from the fake sheriffs who had just removed their counterfeit uniforms displaying numerous gang tattoos. Kurt was introduced by Dean Baxter, the debonair talk show host who waited to greet him on the sound stage. The show 'Talk Shop' was a popular one with a full audience who welcomed Kurt with warm applause.

"Ladies and gentlemen, our next guest has a new book out entitled, 'Sobriety for Sale,' where he reveals the truth about pharmaceutical drugs in America and how Big Pharma plays a critical key in today's American drug addiction epidemic. Will you all please welcome the founder of Clarity Recovery in Malibu, Mr. Kurt Roswell!" Said Dean.

Kurt took his seat, and the audience was cured into silence.

"Now, Kurt, I know that all of us have dealt or will deal with a family member or loved one that is dealing with addiction. I have to tell you, this book of yours is a real eye-opener." Dean said.

"Here's something to consider... So, you have cocaine and heroin on one end that is the centerpiece for drug distribution in America, making criminals wealthy. Then on the other end, you have an array of pills that are enriching the pharmaceutical companies," Kurt replied.

"Right Right," Dean nodded.

"So, what they're telling us is don't use this! Don't use this! Drugs are drugs, okay. Oxycontin, suboxone... These are all just forms of legal Heroin," Kurt explained.

"Like methadone?" Dean asked.

"Absolutely."

"So, how are people to deal with addiction?" Dean asked.

"Dean, I would say that treatment works, and I am certain that there is hope. At Clarity Recovery in Malibu, we make it our mission to cure people of this evil epidemic."

Cheyanne's room was dark as the blinds were closed. A nurse walked into the room to wake Cheyanne, but she didn't wake. The nurse rushed out and screamed for help, but it was already too late. Echo's sister was dead.

The Dukes

I.

It was only on occasion such as this that Big Jack Tennyson would feel comfortable addressing such a large crowd. It's not that he didn't like people; he just wasn't much for gatherings unless it was with family and friends. This was the exception because, strangely, the fans filling the old Albuquerque sports stadium's stands were like family. Even the press agents standing directly in front of him were welcomed. It was goodbye after all—a goodbye to Something that meant a lot to many people. For him personally, it would be the last time he'd be standing on this Kentucky bluegrass. He pulled down his mask to speak into the report's microphone. We've had some great memories in this park; I can remember the first time I sat in this stadium right over there between third and home. Today is the end of an era, but the beginning of a new one! As much as it saddens me to tear down this stadium, I can't tell you how excited I am to open the new park across the street! The best is yet to come! The fans roared as electricity filled the air. The reception was like that of a championship game.

Even though a new stadium was already built, Big Jack still struggled to hide the tinge of sadness in his throat. His voice shook at times during his closing remarks. Colt stood right beside him and probably noticed, but if he did, he knew Big Jack wouldn't have wanted him to, so he wouldn't have mentioned it either way. Colt knows his father isn't into emotions and feelings and girly shit, as he often puts it. He raised Colt to be tough. He introduced him to be manly, but part of him still took pleasure in seeing his dad fight back the tears. He didn't know why he just did. His dad was sixty, and he hadn't seen his father cry once in all of his thirty years. Was he done speaking, or was he just too emotional to finish? Colt thought, as his father handed him the microphone. Behind his mask was a smile that he hid from his father to give his remarks,

"On behalf of the players and coaches of the Albuquerque Dukes triple-A minor league baseball team, we will say goodbye to this old park and say hello to the new stadium right across the street!"

The stadium had calmed only for a moment between Colt's remarks and his father's. The roar rose again and brought a smile to his face as he handed the microphone back over to Big Jack.

"Duke manager Buck Hearst was unable to make it today, so we all here will say goodbye on his behalf. Thank you to our fans and the great city of Albuquerque for all of its support."

This last roar from the fans was louder than the music meant to send the father and son off. The press agents flashed their cameras as the two of them waved to the roaring fans. A smile was exchanged between the father and son.

II.

The broadcast was well managed and provided a lovely view of the front of the stadium for Buck and his wife, Sue, who sat in front of their television. The image was peaceful only for a few moments before the wrecking ball, painted like a baseball, came crashing in. It was an odd thing that his mind was focused on the recession instead of the celebratory meaning behind what he was watching on screen. He was only forty-five, but he acted like he was Big Jack's age. He even looked at it too, and that attitude didn't come from his wife. She was only forty, and she's not the nagging type. It was what he chose to focus on during different times in his life that caused his stress.

"Stress will age you faster than anything else," is what his wife reminded him of always. He didn't care,

"We're in a got-damn recession, and this son of a bitch puts up a new stadium."

COVID-19 was Something that he stressed about in addition to everything else in his life. He argued that it wasn't worrying, but just Something he took more seriously than others. Part of him didn't even agree that people are gathered at the stadium, to begin with. Just about everyone in the stands wore masks, though, so it was hard for him to argue. He continued,

"What we need to do is recruit more talent, there was absolutely nothing wrong with that old stadium."

He started turning red, "Calm down, sweetheart." She rubbed his burly shoulders.

"Sue, it's so damn hard to win games when the general manager of the team has his head so gottdamn far up his ass," Buck sighed.

"Just remember that we need to refinance this house, and the checks he's signing are the only thing keeping us from foreclosing."

The image split in two and showed a montage of reactions from those on sight watching with their own eyes. Mascot Duke danced in the stands among fans who were in awe of the demolition. Buck's eyes narrowed as he watched the dancing.

Fucking idiot, He thought.

A young fan approached ace pitcher Kirk Sullivan and had his Baseball signed.

"When are you going to the Majors, Sully?"

"Whenever they call me up," Kirk said.

Buck shook his head, the image switched from camera to camera across the stadium and captured onlookers conversing. Veteran pitchers Dale Kenney and Emmett Birdsong stood in front of a camera as they were interviewed for the local news. They were among those who didn't stress over the virus. Their masks were tucked away in their pockets, and they had been since they arrived.

"It's like the saying goes, out with the old and in with the new!" Dale said.

The sign language interpreter beside them assisted Emmett as he signaled his message into the camera.

"Mr. Birdsong is saying that he is going to miss looking out of the left field to the beautiful New Mexican sunsets but looks forward to playing on Kentucky bluegrass at the new stadium."

Sue continued to rub Buck's tense shoulders. She was petite, so this was a workout for her. He watched the angle switch to the dugout as right-handed closer Osvaldo Quintana filled the screen now. He was only twenty-two, but he was an old soul. Buck frowned in confusion as the camera captured him gathering dirt from the ground before being called out from the pitching coach Wally Crane.

"Something profound down there, son? What the hell are you doing gathering dirt?"

"Holy dirt," Osvaldo said with a smile, but the seventy-year-old coach wasn't amused.

"You better get the hell out of here, son, or you won't live to tell another confession. They're fixing to tear this sucker down right now!"

III.

James Yoakum was the center fielder, and Van Scarborough was the catcher. They sat inside of an old van and drank beer, their favorite pastime. They weren't the camera-friendly type, nor did they worry themselves with masks.

Can't drink whiskey with a mask on, was their excuse. James was only twenty-two and Van twenty-one. They had plenty of time for it to grow on them someday, possibly. How long would things be this way, and why did they? Maybe they wanted to block out the threat COVID introduced into their lives. What was that threat? Baseball coming to an end. They heard those rumors, and if you had just met them, you'd think that's why they drank so much, but you'd be wrong. They've been heavy drinkers since before the pandemic. Why stop now? They thought.

Maybe the rest of the team would rub off on them eventually. Everyone else wore masks and took the virus seriously, James and Van only took their stardom seriously.

"Tear it down! Demolish the fucking thing already!" Van screamed as he watched the demolition from a window.

It wasn't going fast enough for him as it reminded him of a slow ball changeup. Those were the annoying ones that curved at the last minute. He hated those.

"You know what I'm going to miss?" James asked.

"What?"

"Being able to smoke pot out in the center during a game," James said.

"What's going to stop you in the new park?" Van asked.

James took a swig of his beer.

"There's going to be stands set up out there."

"Well, then you're just going to have to share your pot with the fans," Van joked.

His attention was taken from the demolition by the loud music that approached them. It was Dustin Rhodes radio. They looked out to see the vintage thirty-two, black roadster beside them. He was the team's shortstop.

"What the fuck are you maniacs up to?" Dustin asked as he turned down the radio.

Van stuck his head out the window approvingly, "Son of a bitch! Look, he finally brought out the black beauty!"

James hopped out of the van to see the car up close. "I never thought I'd see this car out of the garage," James said.

"Well, today is a special day, I guess. I just showed the car off to your dad."

"How long have you been working on this mother?" James asked.

"Two years and counting. I'm not done yet," Dustin asked.

Van tossed a can of beer to Dustin. "Hot dog! It looks pretty!" Van said.

"Let's down these mothers and get in there. I don't want to miss the festivities," Dustin said.

"Here's to the old park!" Van shouted.

"I'll drink to that!" Dustin said.

"Here's to the old dugout, where I screwed two strippers at the same time," James said before drinking his beer.

"How come you never told me about that?" Van asked.

"Because one of them was your sister." Van chased James across the park.

"Fuck you, redneck!" Van screamed as James ran from him.

"Let's get this over with and get some beer!" Dustin shouted, but the two of them were gone, caught up in the chase.

IV.

Billy was the Duke's announcer. He watched as the three young men approached, and excitedly announced their arrival using the P.A. system. His job was secure, he thought because he possessed an extra sense of comfort, seeing as how he worked alone in a box. No worry about spreading the virus, what if the rumors were right and the virus would potentially end baseball and sports in general? In the back of his mind, he figured he could find a job in radio. No one could dispute that he already had the voice for it,

"Well, look here, ladies and gentlemen. The Albuquerque Dukes' very own Van Scarborough, Dusty Rhodes, and James Yoakum!"

The fans cheer as Colt and Big Jack greet the young men while they stumble over one another, walking down the stairs.

"Nice of you boys to show up," Big Jack said.

Dustin looked around for a moment, "Where is everyone else?"

"That's a damn good question," said Colt.

Clementine Concepcion was the right fielder and among those who were not accounted for at the stadium. He wore his mask everywhere he went religiously. He did his part to prevent the spread of COVID, but instead of celebrating with his team, he was sleeping, and the next moment, he was awake and staring down the barrel of the gun drawn between his eyes. What was even more surprising to him was the fact that it was his wife holding it.

"If you leave me, I'll kill you," she said calmly.

"Calm down, Franny, tell me what's going on," He said with a shaking voice.

Her name is Frances. Franny is what he used when he was in trouble, but a gun wasn't expected. This was more than just trouble, what could he have done to deserve this? She broke down, unable to maintain the facade,

"You're lying to me!"

"Please put the gun down, let's just talk."

Before she could wipe her tears away, he slapped the gun out of her hand, and when he did, it went off. A bullet ricocheted and hit a mirror, Frances was never going to pull the trigger. She never even liked guns. It was evident by the way she screamed and flinched at the sound of the shattered glass. Clementine was shaken by it too, but he was more composed and could snatch the firearm away.

"Are you out of your fucking mind?!" He shouted.

"If you leave me, I'll kill myself!" Frances cried.

"Do you think I'm going to leave my wife and kids for some fucking psycho bitch?"

The words didn't resonate with her. The doubts still consumed her as she continued to beg,

"Don't leave, please!"

She continued to weep after he slammed the door behind him. She was alone.

V.

News of the demolition would spread like wildfire throughout the city. Baseball was its bread and butter and effected all aspects of society. It was reported in a play by play through the radio inside the bait and tackle shop was Cheyanne, and his father sat. Larry looked at his twenty-year-old son from time to time to check for any new reactions. He was eighty years old, but his senses never dulled when it came to his son. He struggled for a month or two after the virus hit. It wasn't that he was sick, but his symptom was more of a virus's side effect, Depression. He knew what it was like first-hand and somewhere inside him, he vowed not to let it come near his son. Cheyanne was only twenty but acted older. Probably because he and his father were so close, but so far apart in age. He learned to see the world through the eyes of a seventy-year-old when he was just ten. That's probably why the demolition warranted a real reaction. Larry had seen enough of them in his time there and was tired of "that attitude ran in the family. Cheyanne picked up the book he had been reading and continued where he left off. It was about the life of Babe Ruth. He only put it down to hear that the crane had malfunctioned momentarily.

"Did you know that some people thought Babe Ruth was black?" He said to Larry.

"Well, he was an orphan, Who knows? He probably didn't even know. Maybe he was an American Indian too," Larry said.

Cheyanne was the second baseman, and he was Native American. His father was proud of that and never missed an opportunity to bring someone's heritage into question. "The babe was bigger than life, The sultan of swat they called him," Cheyanne said.

"The sultan of swat, the king of crash, the colossus of clout, and my personal favorite, the great bambino," Larry added with a smile.

"Did you ever see him play, dad?"

"I saw the babe play during his short stint with Boston Braves in nineteen thirty-five. Don't remember much of it, but I knew I was there. You're Shi'coo took me. I remember we were out there for the five nations pow wow!"

Larry was stirred up, recalling the events he witnessed, but his attention shifted to the customer that walked in.

"Do y'all sell ballyhoo vac packs?" The man asked.

"All out," Larry said.

"All we carry are the herring vac packs," Cheyanne added.

The customer recognized Cheyanne, as all customers do.

"Shouldn't you be down at the stadium right now, boy?" He asked Cheyanne.

"He gets paid to play ball. There ain't no games today," Larry interjected.

"I hear your boss. Knock em dead down there on opening day, kid."

"Thanks!" Cheyanne said. Larry waited for the customer to leave before giving Cheyanne a piece of his mind, "You know what your problem is?"

"What's that pop?"

"You're an ass kisser. Nobody likes an ass kisser."

"Give me a break, and I'm just trying to be nice to the customers," Cheyanne said.

"Well, just remember, you don't have to kiss anyone's ass. Especially a white man's," Larry said.

The memory of watching Babe Ruth play had escaped Larry. He was too angry to recall good memories and could not see past his anger. All he could think about was his son kissing up to a white man. Cheyanne knew this wasn't a topic to pick a fight on as Larry would win every time, so he shook his head and went back to reading his book.

VI.

"Yeah, and now they have that damn ignition interlock device like that's going to do anything," Blackie Yoakum sat under the sun with a beer in hand, going on about the DWI problem in New Mexico. Two car enthusiasts sat with him and one of them coughed, and Blackie gave him a look. It's the same look everyone gives anyone who coughs or sneezes. It's a look that's deserved and known by all these days, who suffer under the pandemic. If you weren't wearing a mask, coughing or sneezing wasn't okay, no matter how much distance was between you and the witness. You either had the virus, or you didn't, and if you weren't tested, then you better have lied and said you were while hoping you weren't infected. That was the case around the hardcore germaphobes, and Blackie needed to comply. Blackie wasn't one of those, but everyone looked at the sneeze. Each took turns discussing the topic.

"What the hell is that thing anyway?" One of the men asked.

The other responded, "It's like a custom Breathalyzer installed in your vehicle. If it detects alcohol, the car won't start."

"Declan, the Irish kid, got one for wrecking into the Palace of the Governors going seventy. Kid's lucky he's alive," Blackie said.

"It all started when that state-wide backlash took off in ninety-two. After that, the mother and her three young girls died in a drunken collision," One of the men said.

The other man added, "They're never going to figure out that us New Mexicans are a bunch of drunks. When someone's born, we drink. When someone dies, we drink. That's it. I'll always drink and drive. I drive better when I'm drunk."

"You're a fucking idiot," Blackie added.

They were talking about the Irish kid sitting at the bar in a strip club with a pint of Guinness in front of him. He was probably dropped off. His driving was questionable, but his talent on the field wasn't. He was the third baseman, and he had one of those names that strangers liked to say in full whenever they greeted him.

"Declan O'Bannon," A young said as she stripper approached him,

"Can I bum a smoke?" She asked.

What did he think of the virus? Given the setting, he put himself in... not a whole heck of a lot.

"You would think an exotic dancer would be making enough dough to buy her smokes," He said.

"I'm working the all you can eat day shift, sweetie; you do the math."

"You know?" He asked.

"Not really, what kind of accent is that?" She asked.

"I'm an Irishman."

"What the hell is an Irishman doing in Albuquerque?"

"I play baseball out here."

"I love baseball," She said.

"What do you know about baseball?"

"Pay for a private dance, and I'll tell you everything I know about baseball," Declan said as he finished his Guinness then continued.

"If I pay for a private dance, the last thing we're going to do is talk about fucking baseball."

She smiled, "We can do whatever you like, sweetie." She escorted him towards a private area.

In contrast to the dimly lit strip club was the left fielder's living room, Shane Caruso. The large windows let in ample sunlight. This was the setting he preferred while practicing voice exercises in his living room. He was one of the cautious ones.

Mask on at all times when outdoors. He sat Indian style taking deep breaths. He was a seasonal performer with the Santa Fe Opera, his true passion, but Baseball would do for now. He was only twenty-seven. He had time to pursue all of his dreams. A younger man emerged from the bedroom with a smile and wink.

"Hey, baby, good morning. Last night was amazing." He said. "You're not going to be very happy with me," Shame replied.

"Please tell me we're still on for today."

"I'm sorry, my boss just called and said I have to be at the stadium for some stupid memorial ceremony. You can come with me!" Shane said.

"You know, I hate sports," The younger man left frustrated because he wasn't Shane's top priority.

VII.

The team captain banged on the training room door. Inside was Mascot Duke, who had been taking his temperature. It read 102.5. Despite this, he told others he felt fine. There was no guarantee it meant he had the virus he rationed with himself. He was right; some who tested positive often had no symptoms, but part of him was more afraid to find out that he did have it instead of being removed from the team, that is, if there would even be a team a month from now.

"Come on, Duke, open up! The kid has to take a leak!" The captain had his nine-year-old son with him.

His wife wanted to name him Dale Jr, but he didn't want a junior. Decker is what they decided to go with. Dale was more content with sharing the same first letter than he was sharing the same name.

"Just a minute, I'll be out in one second!" Duke shouted.

"Hurry up, will ya!" Decker held on anxiously.

Dale produced his cell phone and called Rose, but got her voicemail. "It's me. I don't know where you are, but it would be nice to talk to you. It's a little sad to see the stadium was torn down and all. I wish you were here, but I know you hate these kinds of things. Well, Decker says he loves you, and I love you too. Talk to you later."

"Daddy, I have to pee!" He put the phone away and banged on the door again, this time more aggressively. His frustration was mounting, "Dammit Duke, what the hell are you doing in there?!"

Soft music played in his bedroom back home, where his wife stood in front of a vanity mirror doing her makeup. She heard the voicemail her husband left but decided to ignore it. She was twenty-seven, and Dale was only thirty-two, but their young marriage had already fallen apart. An older man of forty-five walked out from the restroom and began to kiss her shoulders and neck. She turned around, and they began to kiss passionately.

The banging on the door continued. Mascot Duke ran out of the training room, pulling himself together. "What the hell is the matter with you, Duke?" Dale asked.

"Sorry."

"Crazy son of a bitch!" Dale shouted as he rushed inside with Decker.

VIII.

Play by play broadcaster Billy Weaver and his producer sat in a studio, getting ready to air.

"You're on!" The producer said with enough enthusiasm for both of them.

"Hello, Albuquerque! This is Billy 'the bean' Weaver! Herewith you're up to the minute Duke baseball news, brought to you by Ritchie Chevrolet. It's a sad day in the Duke city; the old Duke stadium's tearing down is happening as I speak. The good news is that the new stadium will be completed just in time for opening day in two weeks!"

He was a pro, but even he couldn't resist the eye candy passing by the studio window. It was a nineteen-year-old woman wearing a mini skirt and tube top. She had a fantastic figure that he couldn't seem to keep his eyes off of. He watched her while continuing,

"Well, we're going to miss that old ballpark. The old stadium was built in nineteen fifty-two. The park opened on May eleventh in nineteen fifty-three, replacing the old Washington Park. It has been home to our beloved Dukes for the past twenty years and will forever be missed by fans and citizens of this great town!"

An F-150 pickup truck came to a sudden stop as it backed out of the driveway, almost hitting the young girl wearing a mask and riding her bicycle. It was Abner Sturgis who slammed on the breaks. His mind was somewhere else. He was probably thinking about how the virus almost took his wife. The memory was fresh. It was the only reason he was wearing a mask now. Or perhaps he thought about the old stadium where he served as the umpire for all of his career. He had his son to thank for making him aware of the little girl. He shouted for his dad to stop. Abner looked distraught as he noticed the young girl ride away in the rear-view mirror. This wouldn't be the first time Cody served as an umpire in the passenger seat, facilitating his dad's driving. Abner was only sixty. He liked to remind Cody that sixty was the new forty.

"I'm sorry son, I didn't see her back there."

Cody lowered his mask, "Be careful, dad, do you want me to drive?" Cody said with a smirk.

"No. These damn kids shouldn't be playing in the damn driveway, to begin with. Put your mask back on."

Abner rambled on, and Cody complied then absorbed it. This caused them to be distracted as he backed into an oncoming truck and caused a collision.

IX.

Buck had turned off his television and begun to put on his Duke coat.

"Sue, I'm going to the ballpark."

"You're sick; I thought we agreed that we would both stay home."

Buck shook his head, "I have to be there."

"Well, then I'm going with you."

"No, I want you to stay here!"

Buck stormed out, and that was that.

Reporters gathered around Big Jack to ask more questions,

"Mr. Tennyson, can we tell the people of Duke city what they can expect from this year's roster?"

"One word, excitement! We have some great new players and, most importantly, a new stadium with all the latest technologies."

Big Jack noticed Buck approaching.

"Here comes the man that's going to bring us a title this year, Coach Buck Hearst!"

Fans cheered as Buck walked down the stadium stairs.

"Buck, come on down here and speak to these great fans!" Big Jack said.

Buck greeted Big Jack with a hug before addressing the reporters,

"I called down here this morning and told the front office that I wasn't going to make it today due to this damn cold, I felt so darn bad, and the truth is, I'm not that sick. I just felt so damn sad to see this old park go than I thought to myself; I told Buck, what the hell are you going to do? Sit around this dam house all day and abandon the team and the fans? So, I got ready, and here I am."

Buck's smile filled his television screen back home, where Sue watched him give remarks. She picked up the remote and turned it off in such a way that it illustrated her frustration. Buck was over the mild disagreement that took place before leaving the house, but Sue wasn't. She gathered her things and stormed out.

Big Jack threw an arm over Buck's shoulder and leaned into a reporter's camera,

"When the opening day comes around, you people are going to get that fever, and when you smell the grass out at the new field, it's going to put a big smile on your faces!" Big Jack laughed.

"Sometimes change is a hard thing to grasp, but what you leave behind is not what is engraved in a stone monument, but what is woven into the lives of others. This team is blessed with the greatest fans, and we're going to bring home more Duke memories to the park across the way! I guarantee you that!" Buck added.

Memorabilia was being taken down inside of the press box by Duke announcer Vic Cappalero. His mask hung around his neck. He needed to breathe in this stadium's air one last time. He stopped and looked out of the window to take in the views one last time,

"Gonna miss this place, Vic?"

He turned and saw the voice came from Dale, who stood in the doorway and removed his mask,

"I'll miss it here, but I won't miss not having air conditioning in this room mid-July," Vic said.

They both laughed as Vic produced a whiskey bottle and two glasses from a box he packed earlier.

"What's your greatest memory?" Dale asked.

"Seeing you pitch a perfect game to New Orleans in O three. You had some of that electric cheddar on that very day!"

They both drank the whiskey.

"I wish I still had it, Vic."

Dale looked down on the field at Kirk Sullivan, being interviewed and continued,

"I wish I could start all over again; sure, I would have done things differently."

"Heck Dale, you're only in your mid-thirties. Satchel Paige was still pitching professionally in his mid- fifties," Vic said as he poured more whiskey in both glasses.

"Yeah, those old-timers were a whole different breed, though. You know what I'm terrified of, Vic?"

"What's that?"

"Losing the passion. You know, the heart to play," Dale said.

"I guess there is just more to life than baseball."

Vic went back to packing. His heart was heavy, like everyone else who had so many memories at the stadium, and he had exhausted all he had to give in reassurance.

"Not for this old-timer, baseball will always be life," Dale said as he raised his glass.

"A toast to the old field."

He waited for Vic, who put down a box and turned to face him. Dale smiled as they touched glasses and drank.

X.

Various sections of the stadium were demolished. Big Jack and Buck stared at the new stadium from a distance while they were being interviewed. Big Jack looked directly into the camera,

"I got into raising cattle back in nineteen seventy-three on a piece of land I still own in Travis county. I bought seventeen heifers from a lady in Texas who had gone out of the dairy business. She'd bred Jersey cows to Brahman bulls, and then she'd bred Hereford bulls to those Brahman Jersey crosses. It was unbelievable. I had a couple of them cows until they were in their twenties. They'd raise a calf every year. I wish I had a thousand of those original cattle instead of just seventeen."

"Experience is a damn good teacher, ain't it?" Buck added then continued,

"I played in the show for six whole years, and you know that at the major league, the separation is not the physical ability as much as it is the mental ability to make adjustments. Adjusting to deal with all the things you have to deal with."

Colt Tennyson and Wally Crane lit up a couple of cigars. Yoakum, Van, Emmett, Clemente, Declan, Osvaldo, and Dusty shared a moment when they looked on as the wrecking ball demolished the stands in right field. Abner Sturgis shed a tear as he and son Cody looked on with fans, players, and press agents.

TWO WEEKS LATER was the opening day. The procession of fans was organized along Main Street in the parking lot. Everyone seemed to be in Duke colors. Floats carry in the team, followed by Billy Weaver and the high school marching band. Big Jack, Buck, and Colt did the honors as they cut the gold tape in front of the main entrance. It was Big Jack who had the privilege of making the big announcement into the P.A. system,

"I've just signed four free agents, and I want everyone to know we're making a push for the title this year. Welcome to the new stadium and a new era!" Big Jack shouted with excitement.

Colt stepped to the microphone,

"I just want to thank all you fans for coming out to support us! You all are our family, and we want to bring home the bacon this year!"

The fans cheered. Colt recognized the resemblance in this crowd's roar. It was the same because the same fans were here. Buck leaned into the P.A. system.

"Let's play ball!" He shouted!

The crowd was even more riled up after those three words. Batting practice was underway on the new immaculate field. Shane Caruso was swinging for the fences, hitting every pitch into deep center field as Wally Crane and the Skipper looked on.

"All he's going to need is a single or a double leading off," Buck said.

"Let him swing for the fences. When it comes time, then we give him the orders." Wally Crane said. He continued. "You don't want to mess with their confidence; we already have enough to work on with these kids."

Buck nodded in agreement, then looked around the field,

"Where the fuck are the rest of my players?"

"Back when I was playing, you showed up early to opening day," Wally commented.

XI.

The sun hadn't seen the inside of the room for days. Van and Yoakum were in bed with two hookers inside of a hotel they likely didn't remember the name of. They didn't give a shit about COVID. If bodies weren't dropping left and right, then the virus would warrant their attention as far as they were concerned. They didn't keep up with the national death toll, and they didn't remember the last reading they heard yesterday. Judging by how many beer and whiskey bottles were scattered across the floor, they likely didn't even remember the night before. Cocaine residue, dirty ashtrays, and pizza boxes were among the trash layers that covered the cheap carpet. The phone was ringing off the hook now, and when Yoakum finally woke, it was just for as long as it took him to yank the cord out of the wall, and within seconds he was back to sleep.

It was Buck on the other line, which had now grown furious because the ringing had stopped abruptly, and he wanted his players here.

"Got dammit, Wally, where the fuck are, they? It's opening day for chrissake," Buck shouted.

He watched as Kirk Francis Sullivan hastily walked out of the dugout to warm up with the rest of the team.

"Where the fuck have you been?" Buck demanded.

"Sorry, coach, couldn't get the truck to start. Grandad had to give me a ride, " Kirk said.

Buck was irritable. Having players half-ass their commitment was intolerable, especially on opening day.

"It's called a phone. You should learn how to fucking use it," Buck said.

"Won't happen again, coach."

Buck had heard this before, but Kirk was quick to answer, and his obsequious demeanor convinced him that it was sincere. Buck's tone became lighter but remained firm enough that it wouldn't be mistaken for weakness,

"Damn straight; it won't. Wally, these kids are going to give me a heart condition."

"Don't let'em do that to you, Skipper, we need to keep you around a while," Wally said.

In the press box, Vic and Billy sat back and read the opening day program.

"Well, there's always next year. I mean, they can't even get their star players to show up on an opening day," Vic said.

"Looks like it's going to be another long season," Billy added.

They watched as the Duke players finished their last count of wind sprints before they hustled off to get ready for game time. Wally and Buck went over the pitching rotation.

"Skipper, he's the only guy we've got that's got five pitches, so we have to start him," Wally said.

"I don't know Wally, I feel like giving it to Dale, but I don't want to lose on opening day."

"I hate to say it, but you know I love Dale," Wally said.

"When he's got that curveball..."

Buck gestured with a thumbs up.

"Yeah, but we need some cheese, and Sullivan's got the electric cheese," Wally said with a smile.

"Alright, we'll start the kid," Buck said.

XII.

"We just got word that the kid Kirk Sullivan we'll start today in replacement of Duke Captain Dale Kenney!" Billy Weaver said.

Big Jack, Buck, and Colt walked into the locker room to speak with the rest of the team before the game.

"Where in the hell are Scarborough and Yoakum?" Big Jack asked.

"No one has any idea where they are. At this point, we just hope it's nothing bad," Buck added.

"Two of my biggest sticks for opening day, for crying out loud," Big Jack said as he shook his head in disappointment.

"I don't know what to tell you," Buck said.

"Well, they're going to be fined. Now let's gather the team."

The rest of the team entered the dugout for a huddle.

Big Jack addressed them, "Boys, I want you all to understand. I know you all got that memo from the commissioner, but I want y'all to know something."

He paused for a moment as if to share a different thought. There was something he wanted to say, but decided against it at the last minute.

"If they hit one of our boys, we're going to hit two of theirs, and if anybody gets suspended, I'm going to pay the fine. You boys will continue to get paid because the commissioner hasn't laid out six million dollars for you ballplayers, and since I'm paying, this is what we're doing. Let's beat their asses inside fucking out."

Big Jack and Colt left the dugout.

"Okay, Sawyer, tell Birdsong he's playing center to fill in for Yoakum. Cheyanne gave Birdsong the instructions in sign language while Buck gave orders to the rest of the players.

"Concepcion, I'm moving you from right to the shortstop. Dusty, you play right. Declan can play catcher. That's the way it's going to have to be. Now let's all huddle up for prayer," Buck said.

The team formed a huddle.

"Father God, thank you for all your blessings. Thank you for giving us the ability to play this game. Please help us to stay healthy and strong. We also pray that the rest of our team is okay wherever in the heck they are, and hopefully, they'll show up today. In Jesus' name."

Part of the team remains in prayer while others carry on.

"Now, let's get out there and kick some butt!" Buck shouted.

His phone rang as if on cue, and he only answered because he was alone now. The bad news he'd received was inevitable. He hoped it wasn't but knew that it was. It was hoped that he gave it to his team, despite the facts. Despite the virus. Despite the likelihood that the Dukes would lose their Major League affiliation.

"Hello?"

In contrast to the positive image of the motivated locker room was the dim hotel that Van and James were still in, only now they were finally stirring awake. One of the hookers opened the blinds, and sunlight rushed in. It was a direct hit to James' face.

"Close the fucking blinds! What the fuck?" He shouted while squinting and covering his face.

"It's fucking three in the afternoon, boys!" She shouted back.

"Fuck off and come back to bed," Van interjected.

The other hooker butted in,

"Hey, you can't talk to my girl like that. Besides, don't you guys have a game today?"

She asked. Van tosses and turns in bed,

"I guess. Do we? Whatever," He said.

The first woman moved from the drapes to a table and fixed herself a line of cocaine. James got up and joined her.

"It's fucking opening day today; I can't believe it," He said.

"What's the opening day?" She asked as she finished fixing her line.

"It's a big fucking deal is what it is," Van said.

"It's just the first game of the season. It doesn't mean shit," James added.

She snorted the line of cocaine and headed for the shower.

"So then what are you losers doing here with us?" She asked.

James followed her into the restroom. Van snorted his line. The other woman got up to join him.

"Fucking opening day, Van said.

XIII.

Kirk Sullivan got ready to take the mound as the rest of the team began to take their positions. This was the first time they'd take in the new stadium. It felt like home. It felt like a place for new memories to be built. Buck tried to get Dale motivated to pinch-hit as he sat on the bench wearing a Duke coat.

"I need you, Dale. I need you to pinch-hit for me," He said.

"Listen, Buck; I'm not a twenty-year-old kid. I'm not going to sit here and pout because you didn't let me start. I'm a team player, and I'll always take one for the team," He responded.

"Thank you," Buck said with a nod.

"No, thank you. Thank you for fucking me again, just like last year," Dale said sarcastically.

Buck was already having a bad day, but this pushed him over the edge. He rushed Dale and pushed him up against the wall,

"Got dammit! Hey, you want to go? There's the fucking door."

Wally immediately intervened and broke them up.

"Dammit! Y'all sombitches are acting like a couple of Gotham children. Hell, my grandkids act more mature than this," Wally lectured.

"Buck pulled himself together.

"I apologize," He said.

"Goddammit Buck, give me some gotdamn respect. I've got my wife and kid out there in the stands."

"Well, get warmed up then," Buck said.

Vic wrote off his scorecard in the press box, as Billy conducted the play-by-play broadcast.

"I'm looking out at the field, and I must say the natural Kentucky bluegrass looks beautiful. The bases look tidy, and I think we're finally ready to play ball! Left-hand sensation Kirk Francis

Sullivan will start for the Dukes today! Enjoy the ace while you can. Any day now, he might be called up," Billy said.

"As an eighteen-year-old rookie, the kid Sullivan struck out three hundred batters in a hundred and ninety-one innings," Vic added.

Sullivan loosened up as he stood on the rubber. The crowd cheered in the stands awaiting the first pitch. Weaver read off of his scorecard,

"Sullivan throws a four-seam fastball, a cutter, a twelve six curveball, a sinker, and a change-up. His out pitch is the cutter at eighty to eighty-five miles per hour with a good inside break on the right-handed batters, resulting in many ground ball outs and double plays. His fastball is in the lower nineties, and his curve is about seventy- four to seventy-six miles per hour with a twelve six straight down break!" Vic shouted.

"Man, this kid sure is something! Here comes the first pitch,"

Billy said with anticipation. Sullivan winded up and moved forward off the rubber to release the first pitch. It was a high, inside curveball. The leadoff man in the catcher's box looked at home plate where Abner quickly stepped away.

"Strike!" Abner shouted.

Sullivan masked his face with his glove as he prepared to deliver what would this time be a cutter.

"Strike two!" Abner shouted.

"The kid sure is getting off to a good start," Billy said. He continued, "Two and zero is the count; one more strike gets the first out of season!"

Sullivan stood poised in deep concentration as the fans were on their feet. He threw an inside fastball. Abner pumped his arm,

"Strike three! You're out!"

The stadium erupted. Buck and Dale exchanged a knowing look.

XIV.

At least the Dukes got to play a few games in the stadium. A few weeks had gone by now, and Buck had called the team for a meeting. Before making a date, he made sure to contact each player individually. He needed to know they'd make it. Somehow, he convinced all the players to wear a mask, but they were in regular clothes. Buck looked around the stadium and took in. The players sat on the bench in front of him and took it in with him. He was giving him this moment. Tonight, they made it, and this night they wore their masks for Buck. This day would mark a change in their lives. One could argue that it was a change more significant than COVID. This was Baseball, and they loved the sport. This is all they knew.

"We just lost our Major League affiliation boys," Buck said with a heavy heart, but it wasn't news.

The rumor of it happening was circling long enough for either town to know there was some truth to it. There were hardly any reactions on the players' faces. This perhaps made it easier for Buck to say those words. If this wasn't news, then what did it mean?

"Nobody knows what's going to happen next," Buck said.

It sunk in for a moment, but then again, it was already there.

"Well, today, let's just play baseball," James said as he produced the bat, he brought with him.

Blackie delivered a baseball and added, "Sounds good to me."

Cheyanne created a glove.

"The way we did when we were young," Van said.

They began to take positions on the field.

"No money, no contracts. Just a genuine love for the game," Big Jack said as he gave Buck a hard pat on the back.

Buck allowed a subtle smile to shift his expression as he followed Big Jack, Colt, and the rest of the team onto the empty field.

"At least we got a new stadium," Big Jack said, and as he did, everyone burst into laughter.

The ball was being tossed from base to base. This was the closest the team had been in a long time.

"It's a little too quiet in here," Kirk said.

"That's because it's empty," Big Jack added sarcastically.

Then it was Buck who started singing a song that only a baseball fan his age would remember. It took a while before the players caught on, but Buck was determined not to stop until they followed his lead. They did from day one, and that's what they did under the lights in their new stadium until the sun went down. They sang together, filled with genuine joy,

"The Dukes are coming out, coming out swinging, hustling all the way. The Dukes are coming out, coming out swinging, action on every play. The Dukes are coming out, coming out swinging, hitting them over the wall, the Dukes are coming out, coming out swinging, come on Dukes, play ball!"

Respect the Mic.

I.
PROBLEMS

The energy is real, that's what I was thinking. It's what I think every time I'm on stage performing pursuing my liberation. It's a dream but trying to get my partners to see it that way was a nightmare. The thought of their negativity sparked anger inside me, but I close my eyes and I channel all of it into the mic, as the words flow free

"Their toxic energy lingers in these moments, like a villain in the movies. The ones that just keep coming back, but I refuse to let it move me," I struck a chord in the audience with those lyrics. Something visceral yet unspoken. I'm not superstitious, but even the birds flying above the ocean seem to dance across the sun rays. Everyone gets it except those closest to me, but those who get it live it. Hip hop ain't about the cars, the women and the money. That's for the sell-outs, but that isn't me. The industry makes it that way for any of us who try to come up. I guess that means I'm staying underground right here, where I'm a king. My people feel me, and I don't just mean black people. Come to think of it, as I'm shaking hands with my fans in the front row; I don't see many blacks in the crowd. Maybe it's because I'm in Japan the land of the rising sun. I don't spend too much time thinking about that shit anyway, just perform. My people are the ones who connect with me, through the music. The drunk, white girl whose security just had to stop from jumping on stage is my people. The Japanese dude pointing to my name on his shirt while his friends snap a pic, is my people. One fan said his father was a kingpin in the Japanese Yakuza and that I would get a key to the city. The show was over, and everyone started doing their own thing. I poured out my energy, and they gave it all back. We are ONE, Kyoto! How are you all feeling?" It sounded like an indoor stadium of a couple hundred thousand when the crowd roared, but it was far from it. They love us out here.

We make twice the amount of money here too; the Japanese are consumers. We had about fifteen-thousand tickets sold as of two hours ago when the concert started. If I account for the tickets sold during the show and the kids who snuck in, I'd say twenty thousand of my people showed up today. That's the capacity for an underground artist like me on the Omi Ohashi Bridge on the way to Club Move, Banba. WunderKind never sleeps and nor do I. They erected some thin rope to set boundaries for the audience and section off the volleyball courts, but I never expect those barricades to do much. I still take selfies with the surfers who jump over them, as I can't discriminate. Some artists will stop a show from keeping a freeloader out, but I was once a freeloader I recall. The way I see it, I have enough money, but I can never have too many fans. Tokyo always reminds me of that, that's where my next show is in a few days. I just jump on the JR line to Tokyo station and I am there in 4 hours.The numbers grow with every tour and so does my movement. As long as people connect with me, then I'm doing what I'm supposed to.

My partners are stuck in the belief that I need to sign with a major label. They keep emphasizing sixty thousand dollars just for signing the dotted line, but they got no respect for hip hop. One label suggested that I grow my hair long and get a couple of tattoos, with one being under my eye. My light brown complexion meant a tattoo would be easily visible. Corinthians 13:13 in cool cursive as they said it would solidify my gangster image, but I am who I am, and that's not me. When I told the executive, he tried to shift my focus to the sixty-thousand-dollar sign-on bonus. When that didn't work, I was shocked at his desperate last resort to make a talking point out of all the women

I could get being front and center with the record label. The ladies are probably already all over you; the youngster is what he said to me.

This was his attempt at flattery, so I'd lower my guard. He knew I was interested in anything he was selling, and he was trying anything he could. His only accomplishment with that shitty pitch was prompting memories of the day I found out my girlfriend of three years was pregnant by my homeboy at the time. I beat his ass, but I walked out of that executive's office before the urge to smack some sense into him took over me. The icing on the cake for his display of classlessness was when he murmured a joke about my name as I walked out. I go by the stage name Problems. It embodies humanity because we all have them. I try not to think about mine often, but I have too many of them. My jaws clench up, remembering the smirk on his stupid face and the anger that overtook me. Those moments seem to have a hold on me, but as this group of excited young people approaches me backstage, I feel a sense of liberation from it as I sign autographs for them. Maybe one day I'll get the big wigs to see what I see because it's beautiful. Time to smoke a Backwood and time to get lit.This is one of the worst places to have weed, but I'm a star here, and it's all good. The kid with the Yakuza dad has me booked at a 5-star hotel, and he's sending over three young girls with more Japanese Whiskey and more weed to give me a Japanese massage. In the words of my favorite rapper - "I'm the new Sinatra."

II.

JONAH

At unpredictable moments he'd be struck as if with thought, and his mood would change in an instant, but at this moment, his favorite lyrics would keep the mood swings away. It wasn't just the music it is what it meant. The burrowed persona of Problems, the artist behind the songs, genuinely solidified this moment of euphoria for Jonah. He observed his frail and pale reflection in the bathroom mirror as he mimicked choreography, he learned from watching music videos. His father spent thousands on therapy with little to no effect at all. The theories of Freud, Jung, and Adler could never help him. Only the pills - which were just a band-aid on a flesh wound and, of course a mask for emotional turmoil. The music and style portrayed by Problems was the only thing Jonah watched or listened to since the nervous breakdown he suffered a year ago. Jonah knew every word of his lyrics and would try to imitate his style from watching music videos, but even with the hours of practice he's put in, the dance style wouldn't be worth ten views on YouTube. He adjusted the volume on the radio to blare the song. There was no one to disturb inside the property or out. Even if the luxurious adobe mansion wasn't so isolated, Galisteo, New Mexico, was only known for Tom Ford and Georgia O'Keefe.

If only he could convince himself of that. After the panic attack, he would gradually reach a point of anxiety that would force him into the extreme isolation that began two months ago. The adobe mansion had become a fortress; nobody got in, nobody got out. If you were Vince, you got in, under the presumed condition that you'd bring the pills he had been addicted to. This was the unspoken rule he had subjected his only friend to, but the tension between them was bearable when the supply was abundant. He swayed side to side, calmly, even though the music was piercingly loud. His head nodded slightly as he waited for the lyrics he remembered to come. When they do come, they come fast and they come hard. He tried to keep up, nailing the first few lyrics, but the anxiety still had a grip on him through the facade of happiness. His favorite artist rapped like a chipmunk compared to him. Jonah was left behind, so he waited for the verse to slow and picked up where he remembered again; he had already lost something only this time. Sure, he could've hit rewind, but that wouldn't bring it back. He says something he wants to believe in the next verse, but deep down, can't. This meant the moment of happiness was coming to an end, unless... He opened the drawer and stared at the pills he had been trying to quit taking. They only offered a temporary fix and the routine became a horrible cycle.

How hard could it be to replace something that didn't last anyway? He underestimated this challenge but slammed the drawer closed always. He was determined to put distance between himself and the bottle even though it had only been six hours since he washed down a handful with tequila. Six hours wasn't nearly enough time to build the momentum he needed to carry him through the night. He liked to keep the lights dimmed, but he knew the sun was still up, making his plans to stay clean all the more difficult. He couldn't shut out the day to speed up time no matter how hard he tried. The large bathroom suddenly felt smaller as the intoxication made his head grow. He didn't know what it was he was fighting, but he knew he had to win. He spits another verse as tears fill his eyes over a sheet of nervousness, almost like he's performing in front of a crowd. He can't finish it. He begins to scream into the radio,

"Liar! Liar! Liar!"

He eyed the drawer for a moment before yanking it open, forcing everything in it to pile to the front. Swiftly he popped the cap off the bottle and threw a handful of the pills in his mouth like skittles. Turned on the faucet and with the same hand, cupped water in his palm, which is neither hot nor cold, and threw it between his jaws over the concoction of pills, not giving two fucks about the temperature. He chewed them up and swallowed even though the water meant to soften them was dripping from the side of his face. His breaths were heavy as the pills hadn't taken effect, but oddly Jonah was starting to calm down knowing what was coming. It was knowing that he had consumed them that brought a sense of comfort, but it wasn't enough to stop him from snatching the gun out the drawer. He immediately held it to his head and paled as he cocked it then shouted,

"Do it, you fucking coward! You fucking coward! Are you afraid? You fucking pussy!"

He would break down and cry after the outburst.

III.

VINCE

"Where's the birthday boy?"

I can see the beads of sweat forming on my head in my reflection on the intercom system as I wait for a response. A dry ninety is typical New Mexican desert weather, but this suit makes me wish I was closer to the ocean. I was done with meetings for the day, so standing here drenched in sweat didn't bother me terribly. Jonah wouldn't give a shit either he knew why I was here. We've seen each other in far worse predicaments over the years. My tan looks darker in the reflection because the lens staring back at me is black. I've been checking my painting since my Uber picked me up, but that's only because I haven't been this excited over a piece of my art in a long time. It's the only reason I haven't pushed the doorbell a third time. Part of me wants to stay here awhile with the painting and just stare at it, even though it's not completed. A bigger part of me wants to surprise my friend with news of the arrangements I've made to celebrate his birthday. I lower the painting out of sight and lean into the intercom system again.

"Jonah, Jonah, where art thou Jonah?"

At first, I hear him clear his throat, and then a flat reply follows,

"Hey Vince, sorry bro, I didn't hear you," he says over the speaker.

I keep the painting concealed at my side as I walk through the narrow but widening space between the two front gates. Jonah's father was a New York City real estate tycoon obsessed with

Santa Fe and all the kitsch art surrounding the art culture. Little did he know that his son was probably the most important artist living in the area that no one had ever heard of. His old age would eventually prevent him from traveling, so eventually, Jonah would occupy the adobe mansion full-time. Jonah stands at the front door at the top of the seemingly endless driveway. The car under the cover at the end of the driveway is the actual Ferrari Dino 246 GT from the movie Sweet Revenge, starring Stockard Channing. Jonah's father bought it at an auction in Beverly Hills.

Jonah's black hair slicked back, but messy like he rushed to straighten up. His posture suggests that everything's fine, but I notice dark rings around his eyes as I get closer. It saddens me that this wasn't completely out of the ordinary, though (I knew he was parting). For that reason, I don't bother pressing him about it. He wouldn't tell me anyway, but I understood. His blue eyes are squinted, and his face neutral. I couldn't read him when he was like this,

"There's the birthday boy!"

I don't stare at the dark rings and instead, try to keep things cheery, but how can I not stare? He wouldn't care. I notice a toothpick in his mouth as I pass by him and enter. Now I could stare at that. I jump at the opportunity to bring up a new subject and point at the toothpick.

"Save some steak for me?" I ask cheerfully.

I thought the intercom distorted his voice, but it was just as flat in person.

"It was jerky," Jonah said as he closed the door behind us.

I usually bring pills or Indica for his anxiety, but I figured since I brought a bottle three days ago, he'd be set, but on occasion, a three-day supply might not last one. That was solely dependent on his mood at any given time. The worse the mood, the more pills he needed to recalibrate himself. I've kept the painting concealed up until this point. Or so I thought.

"Wow! This is excellent work, Vince. How long did it take you to do this?"

I had a slightly more dramatic reveal planned, but I'm honestly just happy that he's not busting my balls for pills. I hand it to him like a new- born.

"It's not quite finished yet, it just needs some small details, but I figured since today is the big day, I'd finally have to fork it over. You know me. I'm a work in progress."

The painting was a mirror image of a Zozobra ceremony. Zozobra is a giant puppet burned in front of all the nearby Santa Fe residents during the town's fiestas. The myth behind the puppet being burned is that all the grief that takes place within a year is burned away with all the ashes of Zozobra. I finished the puppet, but I'm anal about the smaller details, which is why it took so fucking long, and I still haven't finished. Suddenly I find myself angry as I think back in search of wasted time but find none. If I let my frustration show, Jonah will automatically know why and complement the painting excessively. He knows how hard I can be on myself. In my defense, I did run out of that shit green I needed for the manicured grass portion. Jonah examines it and I can see that he's genuinely happy looking at it. My anger is overtaken with a sense of satisfaction as he smiles thinly. This was a rare sight, but the moment is cut short when he asks me the question I dreaded.

"Hey, did you bring those pills?"

I sigh as he gently lowers the painting onto the dining room table.

"Damn bro, didn't I just give you like twenty a couple of days ago?" I ask.

"Yes, you did, but see, the problem is that I need to know I have some on standby in case I run out."

My girlfriend Cat is how I get the pills, but it's a fucking hassle every time. I know her dad will never trust me. That's because no one's good enough to date her. He wouldn't trust any guy with his daughter, and I sure am not that guy. He's probably randomly waiting in a window watching for me to show up as we speak. Maybe he noticed his pill bottles getting low and suspects me somehow.

"Cat's the hook-up, man, we have to see what she says."

"Bro, her dad's a doctor, she can easily get those pills. Come on, man!" He demanded.

Today, being his birthday meant things would go differently, but these discussions don't end on good terms. Never have, never will.

"Look, I told you I would ask her, chill," I say, asserting myself this time.

Fuck the pills, I thought, get a fucking life, bro. How much of this could I verbalize before he kicks me out like after our last argument? I couldn't know for sure, but I knew my cheeks were reddening, which meant he already knew I was growing more and more irritated. Why hold back now? Jonah sighs as his fingers comb through his hair, shuddering like an addict. Seeing his hand tremble pains me as his suffering is apparent. He wasn't always like this, but our hardcore days of coke and ecstasy will do this to a person. To a person who doesn't stop, which is what I did eventually. I was lucky and understood that I had to get out. Maybe my anger comes from the helplessness I feel when I see him like this. I blurt out something to cut the tension and keep the peace.

"I'm going to call her right now. Let me use the john first. Cool?" I ask, walking toward the bathroom.

He responds faintly. "Yeah."

I close the door behind me and look at my reflection. The air conditioner cooled me down when I entered the house, but my skin still glistened from the sweat that remained. I wash my face and dry it with a towel. I had no intention of calling Cat, but I noticed one of Jonah's sink drawers is broken while contemplating my next move. I suddenly clench my chest with sheer anxiety. That was my reaction, not to the broken drawer, but to the handgun he had inside. What was he doing with it? I should get rid of it. I thought. As I begin to pick it up, it feels heavier than it looks. The heaviness is due in part to my shaking hands.

"What the fuck is taking so long?" Jonah's voice echoed through the door.

I drop the gun on the floor, and the clash is loud, but only to me. Did he know it was the gun? I thought. His voice echoes through the door again,

"Yo!"

I quickly pick up the gun and shut it in the drawer,

"Yeah! I'm good! Be out in a second!"

Sweat covered my face again, but I didn't waste time wiping it off for fear that he'd grow suspicious if he weren't already. I try not to look nervous as I emerge.

"I only have five pills left, bro," He says, and I'm relieved that he's focused on the pills.

Maybe I'd have another chance to get that gun out of the house. That thought was dismissed at the sight of his trembling hands.

"Jonah, these pills are only going to have a short-term effect on you. Trust me; you don't want to get addicted to these things," I plead then continue, "Why don't we just get you a therapist? Someone cool that can help you find an outlet for this anxiety thing?" I ask.

I've been taking care of his errands ever since the panic attack. If I don't take the initiative, this sort of thing would never come up for discussion.

"The last thing I need is some shrink making things worse. Don't worry about me, just keep getting the pills, and I'll be fine," He snaps.

"Do you know why I painted that picture for you? I remembered when we were kids growing up and how you used to love watching Zozobra burn. Last year was our first time missing that celebration since we were kids, Jonah. Do you realize that?"

He shifts uncontrollably as I continue, "It hurt me, man, this anxiety thing is bullshit! I hate seeing you like this! Your favorite rapper performed in Japan last night. We could have flown out there to see him for your birthday if you wouldn't let fear control your life."

I see I'm pressing Jonah, but if I at least gave him something to think about, it would be worth the risk of him throwing me out.

"Bro, we're going up to Santa Fe next week, you need this. I booked a helicopter for us, bro. A fucking helicopter!"

I expected his excitement to grow, but it didn't. Instead, he frustratingly rubs his eyes, but I feel like I'm getting through to him.

"We're watching Zozobra burn from the sky. You don't even have to be around people."

Surely, I've sold him on this as this appealed to his mental illness. It doesn't get any better than that view we'd have of the ceremony. He stops massaging his temples.

"Take your painting and get the fuck out."

It was the calmness with which he said it that shocked me the most. It meant his mind was clear and that he's cognizant. It wasn't the drugs, so how could he say such a thing? I take my painting and leave.

JONAH waited as the door slammed shut before he jumped into the persona of Problems and yelled out a verse directed at Vince,

"Their toxic energy lingers in these moments, like a villain in the movies! The ones that just keep coming back, but I refuse to let it move me!"

He knew Vince would still be within earshot when he proceeded to scream,

"Fuck you! Fuck you!"

The persona of Problems would wear off shortly after, and he'd become exhausted and depressed. The exhaustion was from the effort he'd put into trying to believe the lyrics. He wanted to, but his twisted mind was incapable, and he didn't understand why. It was a persona within a persona. He was convinced that he was being lied to as if Problems betrayed him somehow.

"Liar! Liar! Liar!" He would scream as he fell to the ground and wept.

IV.

CAT

What's he doing here this late at night? I hadn't looked out the window yet, but I knew the pebbles hitting the glass were coming from my boyfriend, Vince. I wanted to pretend I was asleep and that I couldn't hear them, but he'd keep throwing them despite knowing how much my dad hated his guts. I show my face so the noise would stop, and my junkie suiter would not become exposed. He waves and smiles that charming smile of his. I never told him that his pearly, white teeth are his most attractive feature. They're whiter than mine, yet he still contends that I'm the most beautiful girl in the world. It's almost every day that he tells me my eyes are like the ocean while combing his fingers through my blonde hair. I open my window, and he starts using the tree as a ladder, gracefully climbing to the second floor. I try not to show my frustration as he quietly crawls in, ducking under the glass. I didn't have to show it and understood what was present. He knew just by being here; he'd be stressing me out. It's not that I didn't want to see him; I just knew my dad would snap if he saw Vince here.

I'm eighteen, but when it comes to dating, he treats me like a kid. I'm all he has, so part of me understands his overprotective nature, but I've reached the end of my rope. I only tolerate it these days because I'm getting closer and closer to leaving for college. I keep my voice at a whisper.

"What are you doing here?" I ask.

"I wanted to see you," He said too loudly, with no regard for the midnight hour.

I quickly silence him as he leans in to kiss my neck.

"Relax, your dad's bedroom is on the other side of the house. There's no way he can hear us," He said, with his body against mine.

"Are you kidding? My dad already threatened not to pay for my school because I saw you," I pull away.

"So that's it? Do three years just go down the drain just like that? You go away to school, and I'm just left here waiting for you to finish?" He asks, with a deflated expression.

I sympathize with Vince, but it's either him or my lifelong dream.

"It's Julliard, Vince. It's one of the most competitive colleges in the country," I affirm.

"It's in New York City. I hate New York City. What about all the other guys you're going to meet out there?"

"Vince, there are two genders on this planet. If you trusted me, you wouldn't think that I'd be messing around on you."

Now he's making me mad.

"You're right, I'm sorry. I just love you so much. What am I going to do without you?" He asks.

"Why don't you want to go to school, Vince? I think it would be so good for you. It would help you evolve and grow as a person."

I'm aware of how much I'm starting to sound like my dad, but I continue,

"You wouldn't be so stagnated out here. You haven't been outside of this house in months. You should see the world now; don't you want to learn new things and grow?" He sighs.

"Look, some people aren't as fortunate as you are, okay?" I say.

"Fortunate?" He asks.

"You have millions of dollars in your bank account."

"Go ahead, call me a miserable millionaire. I'm just walking around this big empty mansion in complete misery. I have my way of evolving, okay. My art helps me do that." He says.

I can't persuade him, so I switch the topic,

"How's Jonah?"

I know things are bad whenever Vince folds his arms.

"He's a fucking mess. He wants more pills." Vince says.

"It's not good for him to get hooked on those things. What he needs is someone that he can talk to. Someone that can help him find an outlet for that anxiety and negative energy," I say.

"I'm not going back over there. I'm done trying to help him," he says, and I can see that he means it.

I'd rather not get involved, but I know I'm Jonah's only other option.

"How many of those pills did he have left?"

Vince smacks his forehead with an open palm, remembering something,

"Fuck!"

"Keep your voice down!" I snapped in a high whisper and continued,

"What is it?"

"Next to his bottle of pills, in a bathroom drawer, he had a gun. I meant to take it, but he kicked me out."

My heart raced for a moment a gun is the last thing he needed. I remember an episode he had two months ago, one night while the three of us were hanging out. We stopped for gas and after I shut off the engine, Jonah went inside to use the restroom while Vince filled up the tank. Five minutes went by, so I sent Vince inside to check on him, and we learned that he was confronting patrons with threats, all because they couldn't guess the name of his favorite rapper.

"Where would he get a gun?" I ask.

"Who knows? With the money he has, he can get anything he wants," Vince mumbles.

"I'll see what I can do," I say, but deep down, I don't see neither Jonah nor Vince changing their ways.

I was only concerned about myself and getting out of New Mexico. Away from my dad, there was just nothing here for me anymore.

V.

PROBLEMS

Usually, whatever I thought about most during the day is what I would end up dreaming about. That was the case today; only I was just taking a quick nap after a long flight. The show in Japan went smoothly for the most part, but the beef I had with security was the most vivid. I was too tired to reflect on it until now. I didn't realize just how tired I was as they day moved like a blur. I can barely remember even walking in my apartment, let alone setting up my laptop, but that's where I sit now. It reads 8:20 in the morning and the day continues or is it just beginning? The creases in my forehead felt like ripples to my fingers. The oil from my skin was left on keys f through k, down to the space bar. Thankfully I'm not a drooler, as I felt I could not control my functions. Fuck security is what I heard over and over in my dream. That's because the security bum-rushed the stage and took my mic. My time was up, but I was the main act, and my people wanted more.

Through a blue haze of smoke, shook hands with the Japanese b-boys in the front row. They got the crowd excited when they started to chant one more song. Within seconds the chant filled the arena, but my assistant was agitated. He knows I don't like to disappoint my fans. The next thing I remember, though, was security escorting me offstage. Before they took my mic, I shouted fuck security into it. The building erupted with those words over and over. Now I remember why I opened my laptop; I had an idea for a song called fuck security. I stand up while typing to stretch my legs. The lyrics I had in mind are foggy and slow to come back to me, but they will eventually. I digress and open the email that just came in. It's from a site for reading and writing poetry called 'Poetry Project.' If I had a second calling, writing poetry was it. The author of this piece is an anonymous one. I pantomime the words as I read it to myself.

They say life can offer the spirit of love to help one survive and ennoble one's life, this is only if that person has the wit, courage, faith, and art to persist, but most of us are blind and live our blind lives out of blindness.

I share my poetry under an anonymous name. I wouldn't want the readers to get distracted from the message I was sending. I sit down and ponder on this piece and the frustration it caused along with pure joy. It resonates with me and creates a level of

personal connection. Most of us are indeed blind and live blind
lives. Anacron and Himself are the stage names of two of my
closest friends, who threatened to walk out on me if I didn't sign
with a label. They were blind and blinded by what the world
considered light. All they saw was the money and failed to
understand the value of change. They couldn't know that they
were signing their lives away. The dudes working security at the
concert in Kyoto were blind, they couldn't see that I was there
for the people. They couldn't see that if it weren't for those
people, I wouldn't be there at all. I wouldn't exist at all and those
people are the reason I am who I am. The security dudes, their
jobs depended on people showing up, they were blind to that. If
it weren't for the people, security wouldn't have a job because
there would be no show. I had a reason to give back to pour my
sould out for those people. My people is what mattered and that
was all that mattered to me. Whoever wrote this poem is my
people, I thought, and no matter if this person is in America or
Japan, we'll always be connected as one.

VI.

JONAH

He paced in the bathroom and chewed up the pills Cat had
brought him like candy. He had already forgotten the fight they
had just minutes before. Perhaps he had become numb to the
reaction he triggered in those who tried helping him over the past
twelve months. Cat did, after all, storm out similarly to Vince,
slamming the door behind her. They never really bonded and nor
did he seem to care. To him, she was just his best friend's
girlfriend. There was no prior bad blood between him and Cat,
and perhaps if she hadn't been in a fight with her dad before
leaving her house, she wouldn't have been inclined to another
one so soon; but Jonah had a way of pushing people to their
limits. He had been made over his, so the price to bring him back
would likely require a willingness to lose yourself. He was too
far gone, and he didn't know where he was. He displayed a brief
moment of normalcy when he disclosed something to Cat that

not even Vince knew about him. He was a writer of poetry a lover of his sould. A false sense of security came over Cat as he opened up to her about his passion for poetry, while at the same time admitting his insecurities.

The thought of having an audience scared him. He only shared his work anonymously online with other anonymous users. It was a community of poets who were free to speak without being judged, but his confession would not serve to be the beginning of the recovery Cat had hoped for in him. He still wanted the pills she brought with her and if it wasn't bad enough that everything, he said was just an act to get them, so was everything he did. Whether or not he discerned that she was in a state of vulnerability was unclear to him. The only thing he was sure about was that the pills were his prey, and it was this goal he had in mind as they passionately kissed. He retrieved the pill bottle from her pocket, but she didn't care. It was Jonah who pulled away, confused, even though he now passed what he wanted. At this point, it was Cat who was lacking something, perhaps this something was connection. It wasn't until he accused her of betraying Vince that she realized there was no connection to be had under his roof. His mind had not pondered these things. No, his reason was somewhere unknown, even to him. He stood perfectly still, hunched over the bathroom faucet as the drugs kicked in. It's where he'd gargle the remnants after a dry swallow because none was to be wasted. Not even the moment itself was to be interrupted. It was sacred to him, like a ceremony and one that he would always attend. When he was ready and not a second before, he dropped the bottle into the crooked drawer with his gun. Unbeknownst to Jonah, his antics had deterred Cat from taking it. He closed the drawer then walked to the front door, his jaw feeling numb as he spoke into the intercom.

"Hey Vince, sorry bro, I didn't hear you."

VII.

VINCE

I already felt stupid after getting arrested, but I needed to bring Cat some good news if I expect her to speak to me ever again.

"No hard feelings, bro," I say to Jonah.

I know he's only in a good mood because Cat brought him a fresh supply of pills. Regardless, I still feel like an idiot coming back here after the way he threw me out. All because of one passionate moment of artistry. That's what I called my flawless mural downtown, as it was a painting of the Zozobra festival. My only regret is the extra two minutes it took me to top it off with the words Viva La Fiesta.

I'm convinced that during those two minutes is when the cop that pulled me over first saw me. I checked over my shoulder after every stroke (What do you mean by stroke, was the dude jacking off?), but the officer was in an unmarked car. I thought I was good at spotting those too, but apparently not. I was caught up in the moment and didn't notice him behind me until his lights came on five miles later. That sadistic fucker, he had me pinned the whole time and I didn't even notice it. If it didn't happen in Cat's car, I wouldn't be here because she probably would never know. If I don't get this gun away from Jonah, I don't know how I will convince her to answer her phone. My brother bailed me out, and her dad had to pick up her car, so I know things are bad. She even mentioned up and leaving to get payback on her for not paying for her school, but that was before she stopped taking my calls. I'm scared, honeslty I feel desperate really. I know I can identify with Jonah in this sense, as I felt like my own lone wolf. The disconnect is in being aware of my fear and desperation. Jonah is just entirely out of touch. "No hard feelings" he says calmly. I can tell by his relaxed demeanor the pills are working. I have to play this smart or else I will be right back where we started. He could flip at any moment and I needed to be prepared.

The confused expression he gives me is because of the beads of sweat forming on my forehead.

"You okay?" He asks casually then continued, "Not cool enough in here for you?"

I stutter in search of a response, not wanting to say the wrong thing.

"I'm gonna use your bathroom," I say, not waiting for permission.

I need to come up with a plan quickly. I start closing the door and notice the room across the hall looks like a tornado hit it. I shut the door and lock it. Did Jonah do that? I thought. Now it was even harder to think of the right thing to say. Did he use up his mood swings for the day, Did Cat notice that room? If she never came into the bathroom to take the gun, then the answer was probably no. I step out of the toilet and stroll to collect the scene in the room across from me, and I can't help but feel shocked at the sight of the Problems memorabilia destroyed. Scattered across the room are clothes, posters, albums. To Jonah, this was Problem's room but for some reason everything is destroyed. My foot loses traction as I bend down to pick up what's under it, a laminated card with Problem's booking information.

"I'm making cocktails, bro. What's your poison?"

I'm startled at the sound of Jonah's voice just a few feet away. He's leaning against the wall with both hands in his pocket. My heart nearly jumps out of my chest, but I've already slipped the card in my bag before I answer,

"I'll have whatever you're having!" I shout through the door.

Damn, first the pills now cocktails? I thought. He nods and spins off the wall toward the kitchen. I inhale deeply, wipe the sweat from my brow, then clear my throat.

"I'm going to step outside and call Cat," I say, heading for the front door.

He shrugs. "You can call her in here if you want."

I turn the knob, "She's going to tear me a new one and I don't want you hearing a grown man cry." He fills cups with ice, and I can see him smile as I step outside to make a call.

I try Cat and get her voicemail, fuck I thought nothing is going to plan. I move a little further away from the door and discreetly produce Problem's business card with all of his contact information.

VIII.

PROBLEMS

Beneath my left eye is more tender than I thought it would be and maybe even a little odd of a spot for a first tattoo, but it has meaning. It isn't vanity but more about effective credibility. It's something the commercial world wouldn't understand. That's why I told myself I wouldn't take any more calls today, this was my time. The last one was with another hard-headed studio exec who didn't respect the art. Mr. Loveless what a douche name but again how fitting was that name? He threw around the word mainstream like I give a damn. Whoever's calling now is persistent, maybe I should pick up. I let it go to voicemail twice already, but they won't leave a message. I don't even recognize this area code, or do I? Whose number starts with 505? Then I remembered my show in Albuquerque, but that still doesn't ring any bells. I guess I will answer it.

"Who is this?" I say, short on patience, keeping the phone away from the bandage on my face.

I hear the name clearly, but I ask him to repeat it a few times. This is how I shook up anyone coming at me with a shady proposition.

"VINCE!" I would look over my shoulder to make sure Jonah didn't hear me shout, but he's working the blender, and I'm too desperate to give a damn. If push came to shove, I would probably run inside and just take the gun. Thoughts of Cat leaving weigh me more and more every minute,

"I'm looking for Problems."

My eyes widen with the sudden realization that I'm speaking to him already. I try to play it cool,

"Yeah, I'm calling from New Mexico, man, you got a lot of heads out here that are into your music, man. I don't know if you've been out here yet or not... but I was wondering if you would be able to come out here and do a private show shortly."

I continue, "We can pay you a generous sum, put you up in a nice hotel room and take care of your airfare," I say.

My heart races less and less as the conversation goes on. We're connecting better than I thought we would. He's down to earth, and I think I hit a sweet spot when I told him I was friends with his biggest fan.

"That's my people, this Jonah kid honestly sounds like my number one fan. I've done Bar Mitzvahs before, but I've never done a private show for only one person. That sounds like some Bill Gates/Van Halen shit."

This dude Vince sounds like a cool guy too, and he's just invited me into town for a Zozobra festival. I could use the vacation not to mention I always enjoy the fans and the money that comes with it. I'm already booked for Albuquerque however this is something that is different. With my tour being over, I saw that as the time I wouldn't be with my fans, so what better way to spend it than with my biggest fan of all?

"Bro, I'll be out there. I'll come! My assistant will send you a list of all my rider."

IX.

JONAH

He knew Vince would be arriving soon. Beyond that, nothing was on his mind as well. Vince had been vague yesterday when telling him to expect a surprise. Bigger than anything he could imagine, but in Jonah's mind, there were limitations, so he set himself up to understand the real expectations. His idea of a good day was one with a pill bottle in hand, and if it was only half full, the day was only half-decent. He did, however, recall handing Vince the car keys with a stern reminder to fill the tank with premium gas. Not the cheap shit as this could effect the engine. Was he awake early in anticipation of what his best friend might have in store for him? No. This morning was much like every other. No matter how much or how little he slept the night before, he'd naturally be awake, and functioning at 6:00 am. Probably due to the unnatural effects of the drugs in his system at any given time which prevented him from getting in a rythm. He had been sitting in front of his living room window for a few hours. Sitting in one location for long stretches of the day was normal.

He watched as his car pulled into the driveway, but there was no reaction as Vince and Problems emerged from the vehicle. Were they too far away for him to recognize his favorite rapper? The man he idolized more than anyone? Had the drugs taken a toll on his eyesight? Maybe it was the bandage over Problems' face that made him unrecognizable. Not likely but Vince did not have time to speculate. More likely is that this was a sign that he was about to prove to Vince how disconnected he is. With or without the pills this was not the Jonah he knew. This wasn't his intent and Vince started to become worried. One could argue that nothing Jonah did these days was intentional. Given the severity of his condition, who could know when his moments of sound judgment came? Or if there were any at all. Maybe the level of severity itself is what the people around him failed to see, but at no fault of their own. What would it say about those closest to him, if they forced him into treatment? Perhaps they failed to see the signs because they were unwilling to. After all, Jonah took the initiative over the circumstances by demanding more of the drug to push everyone away ultimately.

He seemed unfazed when his laptop was being used by his favorite rapper, who asked him for permission to check an email. When Vince approached him with the pitch of going to see Zozobra with Problems, it would lead to an argument. There was a consensus shared between them to move into a back room before it began, which left Problems to his emails, but what purpose did it serve during the shouting match that took place? He watched as Vince stormed out, not knowing that this would be the last time he'd see his best friend. Problems turned to face him. His tone was snarky,

"What's the problem?"

"Just shut the fuck up, Malcolm."

This sparked a reaction in Problems that surprised even him. To Problems, Vince was a good guy, judging by what he overheard; Jonah was the antagonist. He snapped,

"Motherfucker don't try and disrespect me! Who the fuck do you think you're talking to?" Said Problems, who stood to his feet, the boiling point reached.

Jonah produced the gun from the bathroom drawer,

"Who the fuck am I?"

The gun fired, and Problems fell, taking the bullet to his groin. The wound was clutched, but the blood still flowed, as did the cries of agony.

"This wouldn't have happened if you weren't a fucking liar!" He screamed, waving the gun.

"What the fuck are you talking about?" Problems could get no other words out to respond with.

Jonah briefly stepped into a back room and emerged with an album in hand. The record played, and in his detached mind, the lyrics served as proof that Problems lied to him.

"Who the fuck is this?" Jonah said, aiming the gun at the record player. Jonah hadn't noticed the rapper had produced a blade until he menaced over him. That was the opportunity Problems needed to lunge with what little energy he had left and sunk the blade into Jonah's neck. The gun immediately went off, and Problems was dead. Jonah emerged under the blue sky for the first time in months. Blood poured from the wound and formed a trail as he staggered down the driveway screaming for help. Was it the drugs or the sunlight that ushered in the immediate sense of calm that would come over him? Those who waited to see this day, if present, would know. His screams ceased, and his eyes filled with tears as he looked up at the white clouds floating above. His features found a genuine smile at the sight, adding to this moment that, in his mind, was considered pure bliss. He winced when pulling the blade from his neck as he continued down the driveway.

He applied pressure to the wound with one hand, and with the other, he picked up the package that had arrived for him. The sunlight seemed to bring him clarity as he faced his own mortality. It was as if he knew these were his last moments. He was quickened with a sense of urgency as he struggled up the driveway and into the house. Next to the rapper's dead body would lie the package casings as Jonah had already begun playing the new record. Stealing his attention was the laptop, which was still displaying whatever Problems had been typing. Craning down stiffly, his eyes widened at the sight of his own words. The poem he had anonymously written just days earlier. The poem that read...

They say life can offer the spirit of love to help one survive and ennoble one's life, this is only if that person has the wit, courage, faith and art to persist, but most of us are blind and live our blind lives out of blindness.

Underneath the poem is a reply that had not yet been sent, written by an anonymous user under Malcolm's name.

* You're not alone, and thanks to your words, I can honestly say that my wings are free, and I finally feel some clarity. *

He hyperventilated and dropped to his knees, falling into the blood from Problems' dead body. The same blood that had soaked the bandage on the rappers' face, causing it to fall away and reveal to Jonah the words "Corinthians 13;13" Problems tattoo. At that moment, he would pick up the gun that killed Problems and make his own path to freedom. There was no one to disturb outside of the isolated mansion. No one that would hear the gunshot that would end Jonah's life.

X.

VINCE

I couldn't stop thinking about Jonah's outburst. It weighed heavily on me, but I felt that weight lifted as soon as I knew I was alone in the back of this chopper, laughing and loving the picturesque views of the Sangre de Cristo Mountains, but I'm not crazy. The pilot probably thinks I'm mad but oh well maybe I am. Oh well, Jonah's dad is paying the bill for this anyway. I'm witnessing the burning of Zozobra. I'm seeing all of the grief of this year being burned away under the night sky. The ashes rise and fill the air beneath the orange glow of the burning puppet. The gathering is massive yet I am along in my isolation. This is better than I remembered and I seem to be the only one that wanted this. I wish Cat could be here too as I wanted to reconnect. When I stopped by her place, it was just to drop off a portrait I painted of her. I knew she wouldn't come to the door but did what I had to do. I left it with her dad, whose tone suggested that she had already left. He didn't need to say it directly, and I didn't need to ask. I knew this day was the beginning of something new. I find myself content with knowing that her dad has a piece of my art in his possession. Maybe his mind will change after seeing how talented I am. I'm not sure exactly what he thought of me before; I just know he didn't like me, but maybe now he'll see how much I love Cat. Perhaps he'll send her the portrait and maybe I can win her back. That's what I want, but I know that it has to be his decision. My eyes are tingly at the thought of Cat being far away. Wherever she is, I know she'll do well. A new beginning, a new beginning, a new beginning. I remind myself. It's easier to keep the tears back this way. The pilot pulls the collective up, and we ascend in preparation to circle the festival for the last time. My only thought now... I wish Jonah could see this.

Valle De Guadalupe

I.

They thought Baja's wine region would be the perfect Getaway. It was the contrast they needed after living in the big city. Vince was a sommelier and had always wanted to make the trek. Although he'd been sober for more than three years, he still appreciated the aesthetic value of viticulture.

"When I was a drinker, I only drank Champagne and Barolo's." Vince utters.

This was more-so the contrast Adrian needed. This is what her husband thought as she lay asleep in the car next to him. He'd also admire her classical beauty. The thought of it made him smile. She was twenty-eight years old, but city life gave her wisdom beyond her years. That's what Vince would tell her from time to time. He attempted to help her focus on the bright side of a short life, but she often reminded him of its fatigue. That's why he empathized with her and ultimately let her take the wheel when it was time to decide on where they'd relocate. He also understood that she knew what was best for their daughter. Not because he was a bad father, but because a mother's connection with a child is the strongest of all. Their daughter Helena was only six. Vince knew she would be like her mother overall, but Helena had his curiosity. That's why it was Adrian who disciplined her as Vince felt at times lost. Curiosity is the only thing she'd be guilty of. Adrian didn't take wondering off lightly and Vince at times would even step in to calm her down when he thought she overreacted. A thought Vince kept to himself was the point of pride he had felt for allowing his wife to make big decisions in their marriage.

He'd express it in other ways though the ways that he knew how. Flowers, chocolates, and even though he couldn't scramble an egg, he'd even make dinner for her sometimes. Usually, it was green chile chicken enchiladas. A recipe he perfected over time, almost to the point of being half way decent. The key ingredient was cream of mushroom. He knew she'd be polite in her critique, but he'd hoped his dishes were not so bad that she'd regret it afterward. He became irritable with the winding roads as they reached the last stretch. Transitioning from straight, four-lane roads to mountain highways would take some getting used to and a lot of patience, which he had proven to possess throughout their seven-year marriage. It kept him young and interested in a boring world. He was thirty but played with their daughter like he was her age. They shared not only the same energy but the same blue eyes. Adrian's eyes were brown, but her hair was long and blonde, which was just a few shades lighter than Vincent's. Helena's hair was a shade in between. The scenery wasn't appealing to her, so she fell asleep in the backseat. Trees along the road and the occasional Gray fox crossing it wouldn't be enough to hold her attention. Still, Vincent's eyes would see hers in the rear-view mirror for the first time since her nap when she woke in a panic and began hyperventilating.

The abrupt stop woke Adrian, who wasted no time tending to their daughter. It didn't matter that they had stopped in a gas station parking lot; she and Vince got out and rushed the backseat. This was a routine that they had become accustomed to. Adrian and Vincent, oddly enough, were roughly the same height. Adrian's legs were long like here frame. Vincent lost his athleticism but was still firm at one-hundred and eighty pounds,

"Breathe! Just take a long deep breath. It's okay; mommy is here with you. Breathe, baby; it's okay." Vincent checks the trunk for water but finds none.

"I'm going to get water!" Adrian reassured Helena as Vincent ran into the gas station.

It was empty, small, and not someplace you'd want to stop for snacks. The gas you could trust, but nothing else.

"Sir, do you have bottled water?!" Vincent preferred figuring things out on his own, but he only saw throwback sodas in dusty glass bottles when he looked around.

What was more annoying is that the older man working the counter had ignored him and occupied fishing lures.

"Sir!" Vincent's temper had no regard for store policy.

He snatched a jug sitting on the counter and stormed outside, where he followed a hose to the back of the shop. The water was clean enough for Helena to drink. The older man observed the situation and refrained from letting his temper get the best of him. He kept his distance and let Vincent finish his business. From where he stood, he could only see Vincent,

"I'm going to need that water jug back." Vincent let out a sigh.

Helena's breathing was back to normal, but he was still angry and needed to set a good example for his family.

"I'm sorry, sir, my daughter was hyperventilating."

"Well, that water should do the trick. It's clean, fresh, and straight from the river up yonder." The older man was polite despite Vincent's odd behavior.

"That's my wife and daughter right over there in the car there."

"I see, we'll. I hope you enjoy these parts."

"Well, I only brought the family here because I've heard good things."

The conversation appears to wrap up, but the older man sends one more question his way,

"What does your family have planned?"

"We're relocating here. Taking a break from city life."

The older man is taken aback,

"You're moving here to live?"

"We just bought a wine vineyard right down the road."

"The Gemini vineyard?"

"That's the one!" Vincent expected the man to share his enthusiasm, but instead, he began to walk back to the shop without a word.

This stuck with Vincent long after they left the gas station and even as they stood across from the vineyard owners. Why was there trepidation in the man's demeanor after I confirmed that this is where we'd stay? He saw no reason for it and could not make sense of the behavior. The owner's Morris and Zia seemed perfectly normal. Morris was fifty-seven and shared the enthusiasm he expected to see in the old gas station owner. He was a handsome, Gray-haired, bohemian dressed in the attire of a yoga master. Zia, who was thirty, was a warm, blond beauty with alluring eyes. She looked like a Woodstock beauty that stepped out of grainy sixteen-millimeter footage to life in high definition. Vincent wasn't good at hiding his attraction toward her, but it wasn't a blatant display either. Adrian wouldn't have hesitated to give him a piece of her mind if she saw it fit to do so. Right now, her mind was in a state of panic because she couldn't find,

"Helena!" She scanned the landscape.

Sounds of rushing water overwhelmed the calm serenity.

"Helena!"

She frantically ran around directionless until she saw the river. Her instincts took her to it. She knew the water would be louder the closer she got to it, and if Helena were here, she wouldn't be able to hear her calling. Vincent had been calm at first, but her cries for Helene rippled throughout the land and triggered him, Morris, and Zia, to all run with her in search of the little girl. It was Adrian who first heard Helena's peppy voice rise of the rushing waters.

"Mommy! Did you see that boy? He was showing me how to skip stones!"

"Helena, you cannot just immediately run off until we go over some ground rules."

Vincent and Zia are relieved as Adrian reprimands Helena.

"Look at me, Helena. It's okay to play, but there are many places and things that could hurt you here. You must be careful. We have to do a walk around and talk about where the safe zones are, okay?"

Her reprimand is interrupted by Morris, who was last to arrive and out of breath.

"Get out! Stay out of that water!"

Vincent helped Adrian and Helena out of the arroyo. Vincent questioned Zia, who laughed for no apparent reason.

"No one goes in there. Are you crazy?" Zia asked.

"Why? What's wrong?" Vincent asked.

"Just stay out of that river, I'll explain when the time is right," Morris said as he walked toward the river, but Adrian wasn't satisfied,

"No. I think you should explain right now."

Morris picked up a stick and drew a line in the dirt.

"Everything on this side of the land belongs to you. Everything on that side of the line does not. For your safety, madam, please stay out of that river., Trust me. As I just said before, I will explain later."

Adrian wouldn't be content until she got the explanation she was owed. Helena was in her new room asleep as Vincent and Adrian talked beside a lantern on a makeshift dining table.

"I don't know if this was such a good idea... For Helena, I mean." Adrian said.

"You mean maybe not a good idea for you."

Vincent knew when Adrian was using Helena's name in place of her own.

"Vince, I'm just not sure it's such a safe place for her. Don't you feel it's a little too isolated?"

"Look Hun, Helena is old enough to understand the difference between a river and a stream. Tomorrow we'll all walk around the property together and go over safe and unsafe zones with her, okay?" Vincent said.

Vincent reaches over to comfort her.

"We're approaching the formative years of our daughter's childhood. She's going to remember this experience for the rest of her life. This is everything we've ever wanted, right?"

Rain began to pour as Adrian pondered her answer.

"Well, it is beautiful here."

They began to kiss and caress each other, but Vincent froze to a halt before things escalated.

"What's wrong?" She asked with genuine concern.

"Let's just try and get a good night's sleep," He said while moving into the bedroom.

Adrian couldn't sleep as her frustrations from the day continued to build. She remained seated at the dining table and watched the rain run down the window. The thunder sounds resembled more of a human cry, and Adrian couldn't help but notice the peculiar sound and moved closer for a look outside. All her eyes could comprehend in the darkness, and though the rain was a lantern about fifty yards away. Probably because it was identical to the one, she was just sitting beside. Then the visage of an older woman is revealed as the lantern is raised, but Adrian still doesn't know what to make of this. As if it were just a figment of her imagination, Adrian closed the blinds. She thought it would be best to gather her things and just went to bed, but curiosity wouldn't let her leave the room. When she reopened the blinds, her heart nearly leaped from her chest at the sight of the older woman who was now just an inch from the window. The eighty-year-old woman frightened Adrian, who screamed at the sight of her. In a blink, the blinds were closed, the front door was locked, and Adrian was in the master bedroom, waking Vincent. When he rushed outside at her request, it was only the pounding rain that he found. This led to an argument that would end with Vincent learning of Adrian's medication deficiency. She stopped taking her pills, and this wasn't the first time. For this reason, she wouldn't be able to convince Adrian of what she saw. Now it was all brought into question, Was any of it real? The door slammed, and Vincent stood alone with a pill bottle in hand. Even though he was right, he felt as though she had won, and while she slept that night, the older woman, if real, had watched her through a window yet again.

II.

All is still and quiet at dawn as the sun shines over the flat field of greenery overlooking the vineyard. It was the sound of knocking at the front door that woke Adrian. Before answering, she checked in on Helena, who was still sound asleep. This brought a smile to her face, seeing her daughter. The sight of Helena resting peacefully had made up for everything that came before it.

At the door was the older woman skulking the premises the previous night. Her features were intense, and her hair was long and gray.

"Good morning I live in a house near the river. My name is Lupe."

"You're the woman from last night?" Adrian asked.

"Yes, I'm sorry if I startled you last night. No one told me you were coming."

Adrian reluctantly took the basket of cookies Lupe handed her, suspecting it was meant to serve as a distraction.

"Morris didn't notify us of any nearby neighbors on the vineyard." Said Adrian.

"You know it was late, and I did look inside without announcing myself, but I noticed a light was on and saw the car in the driveway. I just wanted to make sure everything was okay."

Her story was enough for Adrian to relax. Her tone changed.

"That's okay I think I was a bit edgy last night. It was late," Adrian said as she lifted a cookie from the basket and unconsciously took a small bite.

"These are yummy! What do you call them?"

"Homemade Biscochitos," Lupe said.

"They're delicious. Thank you."

"The secret is the anise and the cinnamon."

Adrian wasted no time moving to the sink to rinse her mouth. She had been allergic to cinnamon, but Lupe stopped her from drinking from the faucet,

"Oh no, dear, you don't want to drink that water. You'll want to take a look at the good pump."

"I'm allergic to cinnamon."

"Well, I didn't put too much."

"I guess one won't kill me. Where is the water source on the property?" Adrian asked.

"El Río de Las Trampas."

"I'm sorry, my Spanish is evil."

"The River of Traps," said Lupe. This intrigued Adrian.

"What about diseases, Giardia that sort of thing?"

"Not this high up All the nasty stuff is always further downstream. You're safe up here... as far as water anyway."

Adrian's intrigue turned into suspicion,

"What's that supposed to mean?"

The meeting with the neighbor had ultimately rubbed Adrian the wrong way. She never answered her question and didn't like that Lupe gave Helena a cookie without getting her permission. Adrian went on about her day but had kept a record that both Morris and Lupe had acted strangely toward her. She wouldn't bother sharing this with Vincent because she thought he'd just bring up the medication again. She contemplated whether or not it would be a good idea while it was just her and Helena at home. Everyone else had raced off to the hospital. Vincent complained about the broken tractor, and while trying to fix it, Morris cut off his finger. Vincent helped him apply pressure to stop the bleeding while Zia did the driving. She could somehow roll a marijuana cigarette at the same time. When it was completed, she took a hit and passed it to Vince, who took a hit. It was like they needed the release more than Morris,

"Vincent, can you hand me the backpack in the backseat?"

Vincent retrieved it and passed the cigarette back to her.

"Look around in there for a box." Zia said.

Vincent produced the strange looking box and then from the backseat held the wheel steady as Zia took the box. He'd never done anything like this before.

"What exactly are you doing?" Vincent asked.

She produced a pipe and held it to Morris' lips then lit a flame to the foil.

"Take the pain away baby!" He shouted as he smoked the pipe.

"What are you giving him? Is that coke?" Vincent asked.

"No, DMT! We have to get him into a psychedelic state before we get to the hospital. Morris hates hospitals." Zia explained.

Morris began to calm down and gaze out of the window. Vincent was concerned that somehow doctors would detect the substance, and Morris would be denied care. It was quite the opposite as he was admitted with ease. Morris stayed overnight, and Zia drove him back to the vineyard. Vincent was somewhat surprised that the doctor's snarky tone didn't upset her more. They tried to find out if retrieving Morris' finger would be worth the trouble. It turns out it wouldn't be, but Vincent wanted to find it anyway. Something in him wanted to prove the Doctor wrong. This thought escaped him for now because while getting high with Zia, they passed by a pale figure on the winding road home. It was, in fact, Vincent's son, but just an apparition. He died some years ago and he tried to push it out of his mind. This was a memory he had locked away and one that would rear its ugly head unexpectedly. It was like the high had left him in an instant as they stood on the side of the road after he slammed on the brakes. His memory was foggy, and he couldn't recall. He remembered his son, of course, but how did he get here? He remembered Zia's thighs. She had teased him during the drive-by dancing in the car, but all he remembered before that was the hospital. Adding to his broken memory was Adrian, who had yelled at him when he got home. She was jealous of Zia and Vincent wasn't the only one who had taken notice of her undeniable beauty. He went straight to sleep that night.

Adrian furiously called out to Helena as she stumbled upon Lupe's property. The house had an old rustic look to it, set in a rural background near the rivers' edge. There was no sign of Helena anywhere, but then an odd sound for this time of night had reached her ears. It was the sound of children playing.

"Helena!" She called.

"Helena, come over here right now!"

She finally spotted Helena running toward her from the side of the dark house. Behind her was Lupe's forty-year-old son, Harp, who videotaped her as she ran to Adrian. His demeanor was that of a child lost in his actions oblivious to everyone. This creeped Adrian out even more than the camera he was holding.

"We were just playing."

"She is not to leave our house. Please bring her to me if she wanders off here, I would also appreciate it if you didn't film my daughter with your camera."

"But we were only playing."

There was no getting through to this guy. Adrian shook her head as she walked away, keeping her voice low as she reprimanded Helena,

"Why do you keep running off like this? You cannot leave the house without me. Is that clear? Why are you doing this?"

Helena hit Adrian square in the face and ran off again, this time towards the river. She was taken aback for a moment before she rushed off after her. Helena had gotten far in a short period and noticed a natural watercourse had flowed toward a young boy who flailed his arms against it. The splashing was in stark contrast to the rest of the calm waters. His eerie howls were heard in the distance as he struggled to breathe. Helena jumped in to save the boy she thought she saw, but after Adrian pulled her from the water, she couldn't recall anything about him other than the fact that his skin was pale.

III.

"How long have you and your old lady been married?" Zia asked Vincent who nervously paced the hospital lobby.

"Three years."

He tried to keep his responses short like he did with Adrian whenever he wasn't in a talking mood, but there was something about Zia that made Vincent submit to her inquiries.

"Is it everything you thought it would be?" She asked, and he pondered for a moment.

"It takes some work, but we're both happy, especially now that we're finally here, and we can start our dream."

"Isn't it a great feeling to know you have something to stand for in this crazy world?"

She said with a smile.

"Yeah, we just wanted to get out of the city life. Live an old-fashioned lifestyle. A simple life."

"Is that what Adrian wants?"

Vincent sensed that Zia wasn't satisfied with his answer.

"What do you mean? She's going to be helping me. You know, like a homemaker. Taking care of our daughter, cooking and stuff like that."

Zia nodded,

"Sounds like an episode of Leave it to Beaver."

"Trust me; we're going to be happy here," Vincent continues, "Do you think they can sow it back on at this point?"

Zia placed a reassuring hand on Vincent's shoulder. His concern for Morris meant a lot to her. He felt guilty that it was cut off because of his complaint, and she knew it.

"Morris will be fine. He's a spiritual warrior."

A nurse walked out, and Vincent met her halfway.

"There should be a patient here by the name of Morris Natas. He came in for a severed finger earlier. I brought it back. I have it with me!"

"I'm not sure about that, sir," She replied.

"Shouldn't we give it to the doctor that operated on him? What do I do with it?"

"I want you to keep that in your possession while I go ahead and find out what's going on."

The nurse left them. Zia knew Vincent had to mute a call from Adrian earlier.

"I'll stay here; why don't you get back to the vineyard and see what Adrian needs."

Vincent took her advice and called Adrian back, but it went straight to voicemail. By now, he was racing down the road and didn't realize how fast he was going until Red and blue lights caught his attention.

"Where have you headed, son?" The cop asked.

"I'm going to my landlord's house, sir, it's urgent," Vincent panicked, and it didn't look good to the cop who noticed the finger wrapped in cloth in a cup of ice.

"Put your hands up, boy!" The cop drew his gun before Vincent could think.

"Officer, it's not what it looks like!"

"I said hands up! Put your fucking hands up now!" Vincent knew the shouting match would go nowhere.

He lightened his tone, "Let me get my license and registration."

"Don't go for shit until told to do so! Place your right hand on the steering wheel, and with your left hand, slowly open the driver's side door."

He complied but could only think of the trouble he would be in later with Adrian when he got home. He had missed three calls from her, and whatever this officer wouldn't compare to Adrian's wrath.

"Now step out of the vehicle and lie face down on the ground with palms face up."

The cop cranked Vincent's arm back and made sure to put the cuffs on extra tight for the extra lip he gave him.

"This is motor unit K1219, requesting a backup auto unit for possible 192. The suspect is in custody. The location is La Ruta del Vino, mile marker fourteen; the suspect stopped for exceeding max speed. Need immediate transport to the district two station office."

"You're sending me to jail?"

"Well, I sure as shit ain't sending you to Disneyland. There's a severed finger in your vehicle that is not yours."

How could Vincent respond in a way that didn't make him look or sound even crazier? He couldn't and to make matters worse, he still couldn't get a hold of Adrian. Maybe he could be released from jail, but how would that go over with her? The calls he missed were the kind a husband doesn't miss. She and Helena were trapped in the vineyard's shed. It was raining, and it was dark. Adrian was in the process of calling the local police. Her back has pressed against the wooden door to keep out whatever was trying to break in. Helena screamed as she watched the horrifying scene unfold.

"Don't let it in!" She said to her mother.

Adrian tried to keep it together as she called local police. The door shook as an animal snarled on the other side. Ramming into it.

"Nine one one, what is your emergency?" Adrian spoke over the loud animal,

"Yes, there's something outside, and it's breaking through the shed. Please send someone now!"

"Ma'am slow down, you're being attacked?"

"An animal, I think it's a wild pig, boar whatever. It charged us, we're locked in a woodshed now, but it's about to break through the door!"

"Okay, I'm sending a unit out there, just tell me your address as clearly as you can."

It was as if that was enough, and suddenly the snorting stopped. The ramming against the door stopped. Adrian and Helena were shocked, and they listened intently as there was only silence.

"Hello? Ma'am, are you still there?"

"Yes, I think it left."

She crept toward the shed door, hopeful that the ordeal was over, but a sharp white tusk penetrated the door, narrowly missing Adrian's midsection. The phone was knocked away and on the other line, screams along with the loud snorting of the seemingly large animal, as all the dispatchers were likely to hear before the phone broke against the floor.

IV.

In a police station holding cell was Vincent who sat on the floor looking at the rickety mirror that stood across from him. He was mentally in a place that made it seem as though he was alone, but he wasn't. He had a burly collie with long, furry hair to match his beard. He slept in a leather jacket and must've been stirring from a bad dream before he finally sat up awake. Vincent's train of thought was broken now that the heavy man stood between him and the mirror with a jail comb that he ran through his hair. At sixty-eight, the man possessed energy that made him seem younger.

"You got a cigarette?" He asked Vincent.

"No. I don't smoke."

"What did they get you for?"

Vincent wasn't in the mood to talk, "It's a long story."

The man was quick to respond, "I got time."

"A friend of mine had an accident on our farm and got his finger amputated while working on a tractor."

The man stopped combing his hair as if he was struck with a thought. Was this a familiar story, or was it something else?

"A tractor, you say?"

"Yeah. I was caught for speeding while trying to get the severed finger back to the hospital. Well, I was driving from the hospital to..."

The man cut him short, "The man that cut his finger off, he wouldn't by chance be named Morris, would he?"

For some reason, Vincent took it as a good sign that the man knew Morris.

"Yes! How did you know, do you know Morris?"

"This is a small town. I know the tractor you're talking about too."

"Yeah, my wife and I bought the property."

Hearing those words gave the man pause.

"You're the man that bought the vineyard?"

"Yes, why is there something wrong with that?" Vincent asked.

The man sat down beside him.

"How exactly did you meet Morris?"

"Through a Craigslist Ad," Vincent could see that the man was unfamiliar with this.

"A what?"

"An advertisement online."

"Have you met Guadalupe yet?"

"Are you talking about the crazy old woman that lives near the river?" Vincent said.

"Boy, you have no idea. You're better off staying in this jail cell right here."

Vincent was confused, but there was something sincere in the man's eyes.

"Let me tell you a little story,"

In a nineteen twenties ballroom, a decadent atmosphere is revealed. Gold and crimson velvet drape down the walls. Strings of rubies and gold trinkets created sparkling webs across the ceiling. The guests mixed and mingled as Waltz music filled the air.

"There was a place called Red's about thirty miles north of here; it was a ballroom built by the coal miners at the turn of the century. Everyone would wear their best threads; the women would get all made up, and people would show up there to dance and drink and have a good old time."

A master of the ceremony took a microphone and cleared the center of the room. The second act of the opera 'Una Costa Rara' began, and two pairs of dancers in their twenties made their way to the center of the room to waltz. Their movements were lissom as they demonstrated the beauty of dance.

"Guadalupe was a young girl at the time. Young and pretty as he was a shy girl, but she loved to dance."

Young Lupe was meek and innocent as she stood behind a group of revellers in a corner as they spun and strutted about the room.

"Now right as things started cooking, in walks a real handsome, debonair type fella."

Everyone turned, and the music stopped as the slack-jawed onlookers stared at the dapper stranger in white. He looked to be about thirty, and he headed straight for young Guadalupe.

"He removed his white fedora, and things started heating up."

The band and crowd were in full swing. The dapper man spun Guadalupe about; soon, all eyes were fixated on them before piercing screams interrupted. The music stopped, and onlookers were horrified when a tail protruded from the stranger's trousers. Woken from her trance, Guadalupe's breath stopped when she saw the bottom. Before she could react, the stranger dipped her and gave her a deep kiss. She fainted afterward, and that's when the entire dance hall went black.

"Legend has it a kiss from him would cause any woman to faint; then your soul was his and his only."

Vaguely, non-human, animal-like feet generated sparks on the floor as they rushed toward the exit. Men and women screamed as sparks flew like gunfire in the dark.

"And quicker than you can say shit on a stick, he was gone."

The dapper stranger was gone, but Guadalupe lay unconscious on the ballroom floor naked. Where the smart man touched her burned marks in the shape of handprints. Vincent let the story sink in while standing in front of the mirror.

"What? Well, who was this guy?" Vincent said.

The cellmate moved into the reflection shining at him.

"Some say it was El Diablo, the devil. Lucifer himself."

With every word, Vincent's intrigue swelled, but an officer approached the cell with news that he wanted to hear, but at the same time, he wanted more time with the cellmate to finish the story. The cop's voice was loud,

"Okay, Senor! You got lucky. Your story checked out, so we're getting you out of here."

Vincent began to gather his things.

"So, what happened to Guadalupe?" He asked anxiously, but the cellmate just looked down at the cold, stone floor.

"Come on, son; it's getting late!" Vincent was out of time, and the steel door closed abruptly.

V.

The footprints of a wild boar appeared around the perimeter of the woodshed. The violent destruction is over and done with as seen from the disarray of the front entrance. The sun rose over the beautiful greenery of the flat field. Glimmering reflections of the river water gleamed in the background and the windmill gyrated slowly. The sound meshed with Vincent's engine as he pulled onto the property.

"Helena and I are getting out of this fucking place!"

Those were Adrian's first words to him as he got out. Through a window, he saw Helena playing with her dolls. She didn't share Adrian's feelings, but then again, she was only a child. Before the discussion could produce any real depth, a park ranger slowed his green F-150 to a stop behind Vincent's vehicle.

"You gotta be fucking kidding me; I called these people last night," Adrian said under her breath.

"What? What happened?" Vincent asked.

Helena and I were trapped in that woodshed out there while a wild animal was trying to attack us.

"What? What time did this happen?"

"While you were out delivering your friend's finger."

An incredulous Vincent didn't know how to react. The Ranger interrupted,

"Hello folks, I apologize, but I just received the dispatch about an hour ago."

This only annoyed Adrian further. Right now, her thought was indeed to leave, and nothing was going to stop her. Something drastic had to take place if she would be convinced to stay. She needed a remedy, and it was one that Morris and Zia had. Her interactions with the people here had not been what she expected. The wall between her and Vincent was only getting higher. Not even law enforcement could make a positive impact as each were in the own world. Although he suggested that those of a man accompanied the boar tracks, the park ranger was no help. In her mind, she and her daughter could've been killed, but it would appear that Morris and Zia had heard her thoughts because they arrived after the park ranger departed and they came bearing gifts. Vincent found it strange that Morris' finger had been sewed back on so easily. Not that he was in the operating room, but it seemed as though it was never severed. They arrived on a motorcycle with Morris doing the driving. He seemed unwilling to take off his gloves when they'd asked to see his finger, but the suspicion didn't last long.

"Thanks, but I'm not sure this is a good time guys. You shouldn't have brought us wine,"

Vincent said as they raised the bottles.

"Oh yes, we should've and more importantly we wanted to," Zia said with a big smile across her face.

"Care for some Malbec?" Zia asked Adrian.

"You have no idea," She replied.

Adrian wasn't into drinking or smoking, but little did she know that this would be what would loosen her up. It would seem that she also needed time away from Vincent. It wasn't until he was gone that the party began for her. He didn't partake in the wine and marijuana. Instead, he went into town to get Adrian's medication. It wasn't long before Adrian was tipsy, and it wasn't clear if she was aware of her actions while her daughter slept in the other room. Morris played the guitar as he watched the two women take off their shirts and bras.

"You see that weightlifting darling? Now you need to come with us up to Santa Fe, New Mexico, and let all your Gloom burn away," He said.

This intrigued Adrian as she took a hit from Zia's cig.

"What's in Santa Fe?"

"Zozobra," He said with a big smile.

"What's Zozobra?" Adrian asked.

"He's a giant effigy that embodies an old man named Gloom. It's a forty- or fifty-foot-tall puppet. It's an annual tradition there during Fiestas! It's a giant party and if you like to party there is nothing better. We're going to fly up there tomorrow and stay at the La Fonda Hotel, where they shot Ride the Pink Horse. My favorite restaurant is up there too- The Pink Adobe- great enchiladas and margaritas. Through the incineration of Zozobra, we burn away all the worries and fears of the previous year. Upon which the fiesta shall commence."

Morris shifted back into a song, and as the night progressed, he orchestrated the women with his music as they pressed lips and kissed on account of their newfound affinity for each other. Helena had peeked through the aperture of the door and saw that her mother was distracted. That's when she snuck out through the bedroom window. When Vincent returned, he noticed Adrian and Zia half-naked and dancing to the drum Morris played. The scene had become ritualistic and Morris had a boner. Vincent's anger changed the room's atmosphere, but Adrian put up a fight for her newfound sense of freedom. The fight was short-lived when Vincent learned that Helena was missing. The first thought in Vincent's mind as he rushed to Lupe's property was the story he was told in jail. He didn't believe Helena could take care of herself, especially since she had been sharing stories of seeing her dead brother at different locations on the vineyard. Vincent felt guilt at this moment for having written off her stories as a joke.

"Where is my daughter?!"

It was only Harp and a large cat on the porch, and the cat looked to be the sane one of the two. Harp looked at Vincent blankly then stared off into the distance.

"Hey!"

Vincent aggressively grabbed Harp's shoulder.

"Helena is inside, Vincent, please come inside."

He let go of Harp's shoulder at the sound of Lupe's voice. Vincent walked through the door that Lupe held open and was stunned by Harp's oddness. Vincent's heart skipped a beat when he noticed Helena was sitting in front of the fireplace, wrapped in a towel with her hair wet. He rushed over to comfort the soaking wet child. She shivered in his arms.

"What have you done!" His anger didn't shake Lupe.

She instead responded calmly,

"It has begun."

Vincent was confused, but because he had Lupe's story in her youth, part of him was disarmed.

"What has begun? What are you talking about?"

"Helena is spellbound. We cannot protect her without your help," She said.

"Who's we? And who are you trying to protect? What the fuck is going on?"

"Your eyes only see what your soul permits them to see, Vincent."

"Listen, I was raised to respect my elders, but I've had enough."

He grabbed Helena's hand and moved toward the door, but he knew he couldn't walk out without hearing everything that Lupe had to say.

"He is very persuasive. His spirit is powerful," She said.

"Morris?"

Her silence affirmed.

"Look, I lost my little boy to an accident. That's part of the reason me and my wife moved here. To get away and move on with our lives."

"Adrian needs you right now. She isn't safe."

"Lupe, I know your story. I know you're innocent can you please watch my daughter for me?"

"Yes. The girl will be safe here with me."

She handed Vincent a small jar of green liquid,

"Before you confront him, drink this. It was grown right here in this land and nourished by the river of traps."

Vincent did as she told him and took a sip of the liquid before bursting into the house where Morris, Zia, and Adrian were nowhere to be found. He drove furiously after reading the note that Adrian left him. He remembered the words I love you written in all caps, but he didn't remember her showing it. This Morris character has betrayed me and manipulated my wife, he thought. Not anymore. Off to Zozobra.

VI.

Downtown Santa Fe held a festive crowd of thousands amidst food vendors and Mariachi music. Somewhere deep in the crowd, we're Adrian, Zia, and Morris laughing and strolling around arm in arm.

"I have something sweet for you, open your mouth."

Adrian followed Zia's command and received a white capsule that was placed on her tongue. Zia revealed the same capsule on her tongue, and they both swallowed them together.

"What was that?" Adrian asked.

"Molly, baby," Zia continued.

"Ecstasy."

"But not just ecstasy, but the purest form of MDMA. Your girls and I are going to roll balls for five hours straight. Pure love and everlasting enchantment all the way! All our Gloom is burning away," Morris said.

A giant grotesquerie standing fifty feet tall with a misshapen head, hollow eyes, pointed flapping ears, and a shapeless mouth stood above a terrace in front of a crowd of at least twenty thousand. Morris and the girls moved through the man's swarm of really drunk and rowdy people chanting,

"Burn him!"

Over and over as the park lights went dark. For Vincent, this view would have a psychedelic filter as he approached the park. He had already consumed all of the green liquid from the jar Lupe gave him. Things were slowly coming into focus now that he was amongst the crowd. It was bumping shoulders that brought back the memory of him nearly sideswiping another vehicle on the way here.

"Hey, bro, you okay?" Vincent didn't know it, but either he was out of it, or he just looked like he was to the two young men who extended their hospitality.

"Are you cool?" The other young man said.

Both appeared to be in their early twenties.

"Yeah," Vincent replied, unsure of himself.

"You can hang with us if you want, man. We're here every year. We know how this thing works."

"What's your name?"

The man asked.

"Vincent."

"How cool is that? We have the same name! I go by Vince, and this is my buddy Jonah."

They all shook hands. Vincent gathered himself enough to convince the two that he was okay flying solo.

"Nice to meet you guys. I'm meeting my wife here, just a little buzzed from a party I just came from."

"Right on, bro. Well, nice meeting you, man. See you around."

They parted ways, and Vincent wasn't okay. The liquid he drank had started to kick in even more than before. The noises amplified his confusion, and so did the blazing puppet. The burning had begun, and Vincent had lost track of how many times he grabbed a Morris look alike. An hour had passed by, and there was no sign of Adrian, Morris, or Zia. His body reacted as if he had just taken something into his system. He staggered back onto the main road where he parked, and the ground moved like an ocean wave. He stood captivated by the blaze that consumed the massive puppet as Gray smoked ascended into the sky even at this distance. He rubbed his eyes, and the only other car on the road slowed to a stop in front of him. Driving was Morris, and in the backseat were Adrian and Zia, who unabashedly made out with each other with kisses and caresses.

"Get in," Morris said.

That was all that Vincent remembered from last night. Now the sun had hit his face and woke him to find Morris casually emerging from his bedroom. This was the moment he realized they had returned to the vineyard. After he saw Morris and no one else, he rushed out to the car wherein the trunk was a black duffel bag. From it, he produced a Ruger mini fourteen rifle. Morris moved into the doorway, unaware of Vincent's actions.

"What's going on, my man?"

"Where the hell is my wife, you fucking freak?"

"Whoa, now listen I don't know what all this sudden hate is about, but one thing is for certain, we need to work it out."

He cocked the rifle and raised it to eye level.

"Where is my wife?"

"Please, Vince, calm down, man, it's me, Morris!"

"I don't know who the fuck you are, but you're not human."

"Vincent, do not do something you're going to regret. Now judging by the way you're behaving; I'd wager that you've ingested some sort of substance. Am I correct?"

He kept the gun aimed at Morris, but inside he began to doubt his course of action.

"I bet you're not even aware that your actions could have gotten you killed last night. Am I right?"

Adrian appeared in the doorway with Helena. Fear filled their eyes at the strange scene that unfolded before them. It was the same for Zia when she ran outside to calm him down. They all pleaded with him to put down the gun, but their voices eventually faded, and Vincent was in a place of his own.

"What is happening to me?"

He ran away to Lupe's house and didn't waste time knocking, so he learned quickly that the house was empty except for abundant candlelight, which filled the living room. He rushed through the house and into the backyard where he found Lupe sitting calmly, staring into the sky.

"What did you give me?!" He demanded.

"The truth. I'm giving you the truth."

"Why can't you just tell me the truth instead of lacing some weird drug in my system?"

"That's not the way it works, Vincent."

Vincent moved directly in front of her as if to demand her full attention.

"I'm getting sick and tired of all of the vague references. All this mystical bullshit is starting to piss me off."

"Well, then to put it more simply, your wife and daughter are in danger. Grave danger."

"I think I've got that one figured out."

"It's not going to stop Vincent."

Lupe stood and motioned for him to follow her back inside. How did Vincent not see Harp, who was sitting on the couch the entire time? He said nothing as he handed Vincent a camera.

"If you want to see the truth, watch it. All you have to do is press play,"

Lupe said.

Vincent stormed out, and when he entered the house, everyone was already gone. Reluctantly he pressed play on the camera only to see footage of Morris, Adrian, and Zia engaging in open and unrestrained sex. It was apparent that Adrian was completely under the influence of an intoxicating substance at the time. It was shot through the bedroom window outside from a voyeuristic perspective. His immediate reaction led him to throw the camera across the house. He wanted his family and he checked every inch of his house and Lupe's, but she and Harp were gone. How? He got in his car but couldn't start the engine because he didn't know where to go. He just sat there for a moment and remembered better days. His wedding and Helena's birthday parties stuck, but when the image of his son came to mind, it only lasted for a blink. It was enough to snap him out of it. He saw himself at the gas station where he stopped for water. It's where he thought he had introduced his family to the older man, but he was wrong. He saw things that weren't real whatever it was that he was in. His eyes began to water with anger and rage. He didn't know what to feel but that was a strange feeling in itself. Even though he hadn't gone anywhere, something had changed in the rear-view mirror. The house was boarded up as if he never lived there. As if Morris and Zia never lived there and as if there was no sign of them. He got out and entered and saw for himself, up close that the house was indeed abandoned. He checked every room, there was nothing. White tapestry divided an area of the living room. He pulled back the drapes to discover Adrian and Helena on the floor, blue and dead. The horrific scene reveals to Vincent that weeks have passed as the bodies sat rotting. Adrian's wedding finger was missing. Vincent was frozen, but his eyes rose to see Morris, who stood in the corner. The look on his face was surreal.

"Look what you did, Vincent."

"Getaway! Get away from me!"

Vincent knew now that he was going crazy or that he had gone crazy in the past. He saw the park ranger enter the house with the old owner of the gas station.

"Get your hands above your head right now!" The Ranger screamed.

"It was him! Not me!"

No matter how much Vincent pointed at Morris, it didn't make a difference. In a brief moment of clarity, Vincent realizes that the room is empty. Now he remembers the moments he held Adrian's and Helena's heads underwater at the river. It was the sound of the thrashing that was most prevalent in these images. His brow furrowed with recollection as a dark clarity came over him. As he complied and descended to one knee, the bottle in his pocket fell, and it was as if he needed to know the truth before he died. His eyes shifted to the bottle and read the label, which he thought all along was for Adrian's prescription, but the name read Vincent G. Madrid. He had already decided what his next move would be. It wouldn't show the shock he felt inside with this revelation, but to raise his hands slowly. This would deter attention and give the impression that the enemy had one, but before this moment could register with the park ranger, Vincent had pressed the cold barrel of his up under his jaw and pulled the trigger. During happier times, a family photo existed of Vincent, Adrian and Helena, all smiling and in another place was Helena's doll floating in a river.

"You belong to your father, the devil, and you want to carry out your father's desires. He was a murder from the beginning, not holding to the truth, for there is no truth in him. When he lies, he speaks his native language, for he is a liar and the father of lies."

Somewhere it was Morris who had the last word and in another place was Vincent, who could no longer hear them because the enemy had won.

Black & Grey

I.

It is a place riddled with creativity, much of which spurred out of poverty, crime, identity crises, and broken homes - the nineteen seventies East Los Angeles barrio. The nineteen forty-nine Housing Act built the Chavez Ravine out of the fear of communism that was sweeping the U.S., while the loud voices of LA cried out for socialism. The result was an opportunity for Mexican American immigrants to acquire land and have a place to finally call home. That was until the government took over, and their dream was deferred. Hundreds of homes in the Chavez Ravine were bulldozed and demolished to build a baseball stadium for the recently relocated Brooklyn Dodgers. While the rest of LA was celebrating America's Pastime, the poverty-stricken former residents of the Ravine were left in complete despair. There was only one place waiting with open arms for these people to call home - East Los Angeles. Jimmy Mills wasn't pale, but he couldn't pass for anything other than white either. Maybe on the outside, but not in here. Not in the California Men's Colony. He was twenty-nine years young, ruggedly handsome, and athletic with an unkept beard. He sat perfectly still as the charismatic yet hardened, Latino Manny Torres finished the prison tattoo on Jimmy's arm. They had a third inmate keeping an eye out for the guards. The tattoo was of an aggressive looking dog with the words 'Lava Dog' underneath. As Manny worked on the shading, he began to tell a story as he often does,

"You know when I finally knew I was bad? I mean a real fucking menace?"

Jimmy indulged him,

"When?"

"I was playing a dominos game in the prison yard a few years back; before you were here, and I had a run-on-fives. I had four-fives in my hand. Do you know what I mean? My shot and the spinner!" Manny said with his eyes focused on the tattoo.

"No shit!"

Jimmy said.

"No bullshit!" Manny replied. He continued, "At the time I'm thinking, I'm gonna drop that five! I'm fucking standing there - a big-money game! People are watching! Then all of the sudden, La Eme hits this dude five times in the back before he falls!" Manny said.

"Five times?" Jimmy asked.

"Then he falls towards me and into the fucking game. Now the games all fucked up - the dominoes are covered in blood. Any normal person would have immediately got out of the way, but I had a run-of- fucking fives." Manny continued, "So I'm standing there like, 'No! Wait!' I'm trying to get the guy the fuck out of the game."

Manny said with his eyes still on the tattoo. Jimmy couldn't help but laugh hysterically.

"You were trying to keep the game going?" Jimmy asked.

"I'm standing there trying to tell the guys to hold on to their dominoes and you know what happens next?" Manny asked Jimmy.

"Fucking lock-up?"

"Damn right, so the guards come and the whole fucking thing gets locked down. Next thing you know I'm sitting on the shitter looking at myself in the mirror saying, 'Look at yourself. There's a human fucking body lying dead out there and all you give a fuck about is your run-of-five.' That's when I knew I was a lost cause," Manny explained.

Jimmy just shrugged.

"Hey, you had a run-of-fives," He said.

Manny finished off the final stage of shading and although it was a prison tattoo, it still looked pretty damn good. This was nineteen seventy-two. Three years had passed, but not a whole lot changed. Manny was now teaching Jimmy the E string technique that he used for his dog tattoo. Jimmy was a fast learner. He was concentrating as he tattooed a hawk engulfed in flames on another inmate's arm.

"In LA I can get you an apprenticeship with the best artist in the business. He's an old friend. It ain't nothing fancy, but it's a job," Manny said.

"Los Angeles?" Jimmy asked.

"Sunshine and fast women, ese. You ready for that?"

"Hell yeah," Jimmy said with a smile.

"Good."

"I owe you one," Jimmy said.

Manny smiled a devilish grin, "You better believe it, ese."

II.

By the time Jimmy got out of bed, all of his belongings were already checked into receiving and release. He took one last look at himself in his prison cell mirror. He was unfazed by how much more unkempt his beard had gotten, even though it was longer than the last time he checked. He wasn't into vanity but he could not help but look. A guard called his name and the morning unlock began.

"Mills! You ready for the world?" The guard asked.

An inmate from down the hall started singing. Ambient prison sounds fill the building as Jimmy walked down the tier. He reached through the bars to shake the hands of various inmates.

"Flying the coupe, Jimmy?" An inmate asked, but Jimmy just shook the outstretched hands without a word.

"You'll be back!" One inmate shouted.

"Good luck asshole!" Shouted another.

In the administration building is where Jimmy was given his parole papers, gate money, and bus tickets. He took one last glance at the prison gates on his way to the bus terminal. It's true what they say about inmates once they're released. The outside world was overwhelming and my stress was in my head. This is how Jimmy felt as he stepped off of the bus at the Union Station bus depot. It was the multitude of people walking through the terminal that got to him. Jimmy observed the festivities of Cinco de Mayo that graced the Art Deco interior of LA's Union Station as he walked down the famous terra-cotta tiled lobby and out into the plaza. He took a moment to embrace the scenic downtown skyline and palm trees blowing in the wind. It was a beautiful sight except for the thick layer of smog that hovered over the entire city. He hailed a cab, but before entering, he noticed a teenager stealing an old woman's purse. The teen looked to be around thirteen and Latino. The woman was a Latina of about seventy to Jimmy's eyes. He couldn't help but take action.

"Start the meter, I'll be right back," He said as he threw his bag in the backseat and took off after the thief.

"Hey! Get back here!" Jimmy easily caught the kid and grabbed the purse back.

"Get off of me!" The boy screamed.

Jimmy shoved the kid,

"Get out of here. You're lucky I'm not a cop."

"Fuck you punk!" The boy spat at Jimmy.

He scattered off as Jimmy handed the bag back to the old woman on his way to the cab. Jimmy got to where he was going, Fast Eddy's Social Club. Right when he walked in, a twenty-five-year-old, covered in tattoos approached him. It was Cruz Silva and he was as friendly as a pit bull. He had mistaken Jimmy for a hobo.

"Hold up, ese. This ain't no shelter. Are you here for a tattoo or what? The soup kitchen is down the street," Cruz said.

"I'm here to meet with Eddy Mack," Jimmy said.

"Do you have an appointment? Eddy ain't here."

Cody entered from the backroom to chime in. He switched the broom back and forth from one hand to the other. He's an athletically fit, eighteen-year-old.

"He'll be in tonight. Do you want me to take a message?" Cody asked.

"Can you just tell him Manny Torres' friend came by?"

"Will do Come back tonight, he'll be here," Cody said.

Jimmy picked up his bag and walked out and down the sidewalk until he reached the first motel he saw. Just a few blocks from Fast Eddy's, the lobby of the Saturn Motel looked more like a filling station and also served as a cigarette, lottery ticket, and junk food vendor. This was like an oasis in a desert offering immense pleasure. The Vietnamese clerk in his fifties approached the counter slowly, dragging his feet in a robe and flip flops with a cigarette and newspaper,

"Good afternoon."

"What are the rates for a single?" Jimmy asked.

"Ten dollars per day," Said the clerk.

Jimmy counted out a week's stay in cash as the clerk handed over the keys.

"What's the name of this place?"

"You no read the sign? Saturn Motel. Like the planet."

"Thanks," Jimmy said.

He walked into his motel room and placed his bag down on the bed then looked around for a moment. The room serves as a transitional live-in quarter for vagrants, drunks, bums, and prostitutes. The word seedy is a vast understatement for these digs, and Jimmy understood this at all costs. Jimmy picked up the phone and dialed a number off of his list of contacts. It rang over the speaker until a receptionist answered.

"LA county Parole Office, how may I direct your call?"

"Hi, I'm looking for Mr. John Emory, this is Jimmy Mills."

"Mr. Emory is out of the office; can I take a message?" The receptionist asked.

"Can you tell him I'm here in Los Angeles? I'm in the Saturn Motel on Whittier. I'll be here for the rest of the week at least, so he knows where to find me. I'll call back in the morning, thanks."

"I'll let him know," said the receptionist.

Jimmy hung up the phone and sat on the bed then looked around again. The room was laced with stained casino-style carpeting. Knock off artworks in crooked frames were all that hung on the wall. A broken mirror sat on a broken dresser. He turned on the small black and white television and the first images that popped up were from a news report on the last American troops leaving Saigon. Jimmy promptly shut off the television and headed for the bathroom. He looked at himself in the mirror before spotting an old dirty razor near the trash can. He lathered up his beard with some soap and started shaving it off.

III.

Hours later outside of Fast Eddy's Social Club, the sun has set, and the night draws near as Jimmy, now clean-shaven, crossed the street from the motel and put out a cigarette before re-entering the tattoo parlor. He walked in and heard oldies music in the background as two bikers played pool and smoked cigarettes. Three Cholos went over tattoo designs, and how these strategies must be present. Two young girls watched as their teenaged girlfriend got a tattoo of a rose on her back. Beside her an old-time Cholo was getting a full back piece of the Virgin Mary from Cruz. Cody was strutting around with blank pieces of paper for sketch drawings. He approached Jimmy right when he walked in.

"Hey man! My dad is in the back, just take a seat," Cody said.

Jimmy sat and admired an illustration book by Caravaggio. The fifty-two-year-old Eddy Mack sat at the desk in his office. He was a strong stern Caucasian and his look would say it all. Across from him was a frail-looking woman in her late sixties, Consuela Ramos.

"They won't stop, Eduardo, they don't listen to me, they have no respect for anyone."

"My hands are tied, Señora. I can't risk getting into a war with these guys, there is nothing that I can do. We all have our territories and when we stick to them, fewer people get hurt," Eddy said.

"I don't want you to hurt anyone maybe just get someone to talk to them. Painting over graffiti every week is expensive, and I don't have the time. People I've known for years are now afraid to come to my store we are losing a lot of money," Consuela said.

Eddy mulled it over for a bit,

"We've known each other for a long time, Consuela. Twenty years now?"

Consuela nodded. Eddy continued,

"I made a promise to always be there for you, no matter what. I intend to keep that promise."

"Thank you," Consuela said.

"But you're going to have to be patient. I have to do it in the right way. Don't antagonize them and Keep quiet. For now, hold on to this for me," Eddy said.

He handed her a stack of twenties at least two hundred dollars.

"I can't this is too much!" She said.

He stood and began to walk her out.

"Nonsense," he said.

The door to Eddy's office opened and Consuela emerged with Eddy a few steps behind him. His presence demands respect and attention as he enters the parlor. Jimmy swiftly stood up to greet Eddy as he made his introduction,

"You Jimmy?"

"Yessir," Jimmy said.

"So, this is the kid Manny spoke so highly of. I heard you were the Michelangelo of the California correctional facilities!"

They shook hands.

"It's great to finally meet you," Jimmy said.

"Why don't you come into the back?" Eddy said.

Jimmy followed Eddy to his private back room. As they made their way, Jimmy felt the stares coming from the other artists, particularly Cruz. In the private room, Eddy returns to tattooing a scary looking, twenty-one-year-old Cholo kid. With the kid was his partner, and even scarier looking twenty-two-year- old.

The Cholo kid was getting lettering in Spanish that read, 'Rucas, Caruchas, y Rolas, Soñeando'. Kimmy was introduced by Eddy,

"Sorry for the hold-up guys. Had to handle a little business. This is Jimmy. He just came back from a vacation," Jimmy admired the tattoo.

"What's the tat mean?" Jimmy asked.

"You know, Lucas, that's like your high school sweetheart or your homegirl or your first love; and caruchas is like, your favorite song,"

The Cholo kid explained. The kid thinks out loud for a minute.

"Soñeando, means that's like my spirit. My soul."

"I dig that man," Jimmy said.

Eddy continued working on the tattoo while Jimmy sat back and admired his work.

"So, Jimmy, you like the city of Angeles so far?" Eddy asked.

"So far, so good. I'm not homesick."

Eddy turned to the Cholo kid and his friend,

"Did you hear the one about the sailor who has been out at sea for two months and finally gets a chance to stop at a brothel? He walks straight up to the Madam, drops down five hundred dollars, and says, 'I want your ugliest woman and a grilled cheese sandwich!' The Madam is astonished," Eddy continued,

"But sir, for that kind of money you could have one of my prettiest ladies and a three-course meal.' The sailor replies, 'Listen darlin', I'm not horny - I'm just homesick," Eddie finished the joke.

They all laughed, he continued,

"You'll like it out here, Jimmy. Sunny days and starry nights. Well, if you can see past the smog, that is."

The sound of a woman screaming was heard coming from the main room. Through the door of Eddy's private room, he saw Cruz putting his hands on a young woman. It was Estrella Silva. She was pretty and innocent looking. That's because she was only twenty years old. She sounded louder during the shouting match she and Cruz were engaged in. Cruz released her arm.

"Get your fucking hands off of me!" She shouted.

"I told you not to come in here. You're not getting a tattoo. Now go the fuck back home!" Cruz shouted.

Eddy walked in and stepped between them,

"I can't have this in here, guys," he said to both of them.

"I don't want her here, Eddy. She ain't getting a tattoo."

Jimmy entered the main shop to see what all of the commotions were about. Estrella dashed toward the exit and on her way, she locked eyes with Jimmy. They shared a moment as Eddy proceeded to calm down Cruz.

"Just calm down, man. No one is going to give her a tattoo. But look around, I've got customers in here. As do you."

Eddy stormed off into the back room.

"Take five, kid," he said to Jimmy in passing before slamming the door shut.

Cody, Cruz, and everyone else in the main room went back to work as usual. Jimmy walked outside to smoke a cigarette. He lit up and immediately noticed Estrella crying and leaning against a graffiti-ridden wall. At first, he simply minded his own business, but as her distress worsened, he couldn't help, but to console her. He produced a bandanna from his pocket and handed it to her,

"Here you go."

She hesitantly took the bandanna and became disconcerted while trying to compose herself.

"Thanks," she said softly.

"Is it safe for you to be out here?" He asked.

"My dad is coming to pick me up."

She hands the bandanna back to him.

"Who are you?" She asked.

"My name is Jimmy."

"Are you getting a tattoo?" She asked.

"No."

Suddenly, from a distance in the sky, Estrella noticed a shooting star,

"Look! A shooting star"

"Don't get too many of those out here, huh?" Jimmy asked.

"Not ones you can see, ese. Where are you from?" She asked, but before Jimmy could answer, Cody came outside holding a broom to call him back into the shop,

"Hey man, come inside and start on some cleaning."

"You work here?" She asked Jimmy.

A car pulled up. It was Estrella's father, Cisco Silva. A regal and weathered fifty-two years old. His pristine, blue fifty-two mercury slowed to a stop at the curb. Cody gave Cisco a nod before returning inside. Jimmy put out his cigarette, but before he could answer Estrella's question, she dashed off to the car.

"See you later, gringo," she said.

Jimmy watched the car drive off before heading back inside. Cody handed Jimmy the broom and showed him where the cleaning supplies were,

"We're closing early tonight, so you can start sweeping the main room."

"I can do that," Jimmy said.

"Good. We keep a clean shop," Cody said.

Jimmy took the broom and readied himself for the closing tasks. Cody ran off to answer a phone call. Jimmy began sweeping in the main room. Cruz stared him down with a devious grin, knowing that Jimmy is no threat to him.

IV.

It was closing time and everyone in the room was gathering their things and cleaning their work areas. Jimmy finished mopping the restroom then took out the garbage. He was approached by Eddy,

"Cody is gonna go over the rest of the closing duties. Keep working hard and maybe you'll get your station."

Eddy then walked back to the main room to hug it out with Cruz before calling it a night and heading home. Cruz gathered the rest of his things and called it a night as well. He turned to Jimmy before exiting,

"Hey homes, you better get used to that mop bucket. This place needs a new maid."

Jimmy ignored him and kept mopping as Cruz snickered and left. Cody closed the shop while Jimmy continued to clean. A white van pulled around the back of the shop with delivery. Cody rushed out to greet the driver. A few minutes passed and Jimmy noticed Cody arguing with the driver, but he continued to go about his cleaning. Suddenly the van sped off and Cody frantically called Jimmy from outside to help him,

"Jimmy, come out here!"

Jimmy rushed outside and saw over five thousand baggies of heroin scattered around the ground. Cody and Jimmy quickly pick up the baggies and scurry everything inside,

"Hurry, man! Help me get this stuff inside!" Cody yelled.

He led Jimmy downstairs into the basement and the storage room.

"You can't tell anyone about this," Cody said.

"You can trust me," Jimmy replied.

The two men frantically organize and store the heroin in a locked away bookcase. Cody sat as he smoked heroin. Chasing the dragon is what they called it. He conversed with Jimmy about his stint in prison.

"Are you sure you don't want any?"

"I've been clean for five years man. I can't go back to that... Does your dad know you use?" Jimmy asked.

"Are you fucking serious? He would kill me I'm an amateur boxer, you know? Thirteen wins, no losses," Cody explained.

He put out the H and lit a cigarette,

"You're a boxer who chases the dragon and smokes cigarettes?"

Jimmy looked through the goods,

"Where did all of this come from?"

"Long story just keep your mouth shut about it. You want some whiskey?" Cody asked.

He broke out a bottle.

"Anything you don't do?" Jimmy asked.

"My dad can't know about any of this shit. My boxing career is the only thing he cares about. Just stick with me and do what I tell ya and I'll take care of you around here. You wanna learn to tattoo, right?" Cody asked.

"Hell yeah."

"I know everything about this shop. Who's who, the client list, the best shifts... Most importantly, I take all of the appointments so anyone that doesn't request my dad is given to who I select, which means, once you get good, I can make you a lot of money. Get you a rep around here," Cody said.

He opened the whiskey bottle and prepared to pour a couple of shots.

"Let me get some glasses from upstairs," Cody said.

While he was upstairs getting the glasses, Jimmy was left to take a long, hard look at the drug that ruined his life. Cody came back down with the glasses.

"Well, at least you drink," Cody said.

"Whiskey usually hits the spot," Jimmy said.

"Good... For a while there I thought you were one of the monks or something,"

Cody said.

"Three rocks, two fingers, and a splash of water. That's the way Sinatra drinks it."

Jimmy said.

"Who's Sinatra?" Cody asked.

"You don't know Frank Sinatra? Kids today."

Jimmy reacted to a sound he heard upstairs.

"It's the fan," Cody said.

"We should get out of here. If your dad catches you here in the morning all strung out, I'm guessing that's lights out for you," Jimmy said.

"Alright, that makes sense," Cody said as he grabbed his jacket.

Jimmy grabbed the whiskey and the glasses as they headed out into the rainy night towards the Saturn Motel. They walked into Jimmy's room and got settled.

"You can have the bed I don't give a shit. I've been in a cell for the past five years," Jimmy said.

"Whatever, man I don't care," Cody replied as he went to use the washroom.

"So, who was the girl in the shop earlier? I sure liked looking at that," Jimmy said.

Cody re-entered the room. "Look man, I know you just got out of jail and everything, but there are other fish in the sea. That's one fish you don't want to catch It'll bite back," Cody warned him.

He went straight for his jacket and got ready to start chasing the dragon again.

"Not in here, man. Please," Jimmy said.

Cody thought about it for a second. "Yeah, you're probably right," He said.

He put all of the heroin paraphernalia back in his jacket and tossed it aside. Jimmy held up the whiskey bottle.

"We still got whiskey."

Then Cody repeated, "We still got whiskey."

The two shared a toast as Jimmy turned on the television. Johnny Carson was on and they continued to pour each other drinks until they fell asleep. In the shop, the phone rang off the hook. It was Eddy calling, he grew impatient with every second that went by without an answer. He drove in front of the shop in a seventy-four Cadillac coupe. He super eyed the shop and noticed that every light was off, and every car was gone. He watched for a moment until he was convinced that the shop was closed, and that Cody wasn't around then he drove off. The next morning Cody woke up and looked at his watch,

"Shit."

He got himself together and exited the motel room. He forgot to take his jacket as he was dishevelled as he walked out of the room and down the walkway. He bumped into a fifty-five-year-old Caucasian man. He was overweight and stubborn, John Emory was his name. He never said it though. "You're excused," is what he uttered instead.

Cody ignored him as he reached the shop and started setting up once he was inside. He went to the basement and discovered that the bookcase lock had been broken off. He opened the door and saw that it was empty. All of the heroin was gone,

"What the fuck?"

He started wigging out, he looked all over the room, trying to find some clue that would tell him what the hell is going on. There is no sign of drugs and finally, when he saw there was no other option, he picked up the phone. It is a Rangoon speaker.

"Hello," Eddy answered.

"Dad!"

"Where the fuck are you?" Eddy asked.

"I'm here, dad and I'm at the shop," Cody said.

"Why didn't you come home last night?" Eddy asked.

"Listen, dad we have a big problem."

Jimmy woke to loud knocks on the door and he looked around to see where Cody was, but realized he was gone. He got up to answer the door.

"Can I help you?" Jimmy asked.

"I'm John Emory, your parole officer? Don't you remember we had an appointment today?" He asked.

"Right... Of course," Jimmy let him in.

Emory silently surveyed the room.

"So, what are your plans?" He asked Jimmy.

"You mean, like a job?" Jimmy asked.

"Yeah a job might be a good start unless you want to stay in this shithole. What made you choose this part of town anyway? Nothing but Mexicans," Emory said.

"I may have an opportunity working at a tattoo parlour nearby," Jimmy replied.

Emory lit a cigarette.

"I never cared for tattoos. Tacky," Emory said.

Jimmy headed for the washroom. Emory spotted Cody's jacket on the bed, but Curiosity compelled him to give it a shake.

"I thought it never rained in Southern California," Jimmy shouted from the other room.

Some of Cody's drug paraphernalia fell out of the jacket.

"Rained for thirty-nine days straight three years ago," Emory said.

In the same moment, Jimmy emerged from the washroom, John grabbed his arm and handcuffed him to the bedpost before swiftly checking his arms for needle tracks.

"What the hell are you doing, man?"

"Let me see the arms," Emory said.

No tracks were apparent, but in Emory's mind, it still didn't make up for the paraphernalia.

"Couldn't kick the habit, huh? I read your file," Emory said.

"It's not mine, man I'm clean. You can test me if you want."

"Well, whose is it then?"

"That's not my jacket, it's..."

"Sure, It belongs to the one-armed man. You violated your parole, you've been out what, a few days?" Emory asked.

He stood Jimmy to his feet and locked the other handcuff around his wrist.

"Shall we?" Emory asked.

Before Jimmy knew what was happening, he was being hauled off to County Jail.

V.

Eddy and Cruz burst through the front door of the shop as Cody sat nervously on the counter.

"What else did they take?" Eddy asked.

"Just the bags, I checked everything," Cody said.

"Okay, get ready to open up shop. Business as usual Cody, I'll deal with you later." Eddy said.

Cody ran off to prep the shop for business.

"Fucking idiot," Eddy said under his breath.

He promptly grabbed the phone to call a meeting.

"Klein!" He shouted.

A Mediterranean style mansion with sixteen bedrooms, thirteen bathrooms, a hand-carved stairway, wraparound balcony, lounge, and wine cellar sat on a multiple acre block. It was draped with immaculate gardens, a pool with water fountains, and an outdoor terrace the size of a football field. A man named Louis Klein, who was educated and debonair, took the phone that was handed to him by one of the servants on his staff,

"Klein here."

After listening for a moment, a look arose on his face that revealed a distasteful reaction to the news.

"The delivery was scheduled for this morning, not last night. Meet me at the office today at three this afternoon," Louis said.

Klein hung up the phone and pondered for a moment. Detective Juan Contreras was a poised and alert forty-five-year-old Latino. As he left the jailhouse he ran into Emory with Jimmy, who were both on their way to a booking. They were forced to interact.

"Contreras!" Said, Emory.

"Hey, John. How are ya?"

"Swell. How's East Los treating you?" Emory asked.

"We're cleaning it up, slowly."

"Well, I took one more scumbag back off the streets for ya today," said Emory as he motioned to Jimmy. He continued,

"Heroin."

This intrigued Detective Contreras. He moved in to get a closer look at Jimmy.

"Folsom gate? The river?" Contreras asked.

"Nah, he was staying at a real shit dive motel on Whittier-said he was working at a tattoo parlor," Emory explained.

This grabbed Contreras' attention.

"What's your name, son?"

"James," Jimmy replied.

"It's Jimmy Mills," Emory interjected then continued.

"New York originally. Did a nickel up at central. Armed robbery," Emory said.

Contreras noticed Jimmy's Lava Dog Tattoo.

"Were you in Vietnam, son?" Contreras asked.

"Yes, sir," Jimmy replied.

Contreras motioned to the tattoo,

"Which regime?"

"First battalion third marines," Jimmy said.

"I was in the twenty-second," Said Contreras.

"Wow... you guys saw a lot of action." Jimmy said.

"That we did... John, do you mind if I talk to this man in private?"

Emory was torn of confusion and so was Jimmy.

"I guess so, but you'd better hurry. I'd like to book him quickly so I can beat traffic," Emory said.

"This won't take but a few minutes," said Contreras.

Emory trailed the men as they walked into an interrogation room.

"Please, John- in private," Contreras pleaded.

"Don't believe anything that punk says, Contreras. He's a junkie," Emory warned.

Inside the interrogation room, Contreras remained standing while Jimmy sat.

"So, you were a lava dog, huh?" Contreras asked.

"Yes, sir. For better or worse," Jimmy replied.

Contreras silently sized Jimmy up.

"You made it out of Vietnam. What the hell are you doing here?"

"When I came back home from Nam, I went back to New York and couldn't deal with it. Heroin was easy to get," Jimmy said.

"The drugs I can almost understand, but armed robbery?"

"I was sick of being treated like a second-class citizen. I couldn't get a job, no real skills. I started working for the Westies. Nobody cares about us, you know. The mob made me feel like someone," Jimmy continued,

"Besides, after four years of taking orders to kill innocent people in the jungle, working for them was easy."

"What's your business in LA?" Contreras asked.

"I learned how to ink in the joint. It's the only skill I have that's legal. My bunk-mate set me up with a job at a parlor in East LA."

"At Fast Eddy's?" Contreras asked.

Jimmy was taken aback, "Yes."

"Do you know who Eddy Mack is?" Contreras asked.

"Not really. Just met him," Jimmy said.

"I've been building a case on Mack and his crew for over a year now. He may be talented and charming, but deep down, he's ruthless. He doesn't care if anyone gets hurt- kids, whoever... He has no regard for anyone but his own. He's taking away hope from people that had very little of it in the first place," Contreras said.

Bewildered by what he had just heard, Jimmy took a deep breath and tried to process everything. Contreras offered Jimmy a cigarette, but he declined.

"Listen, Jimmy, I don't know you, but I think you deserve a fair shot. I can get you out of here, but I'm going to need you to help me. You can help me bring down these animals."

A knock on the door interrupted them.

"Hold that thought," Contreras said.

He took a moment and stepped outside then closed the door behind him. Emory waited impatiently outside the door.

"What the hell is going on in there?" Emory asked.

"Listen, I'm gonna need this kid. I can use him on a case," Contreras said.

"No way. He's a loser, Juan. I'm going to put him where he belongs," Emory said.

"What are the charges?" Contreras asked.

"He had a felony amount of heroin on him, in violation of his parole. He's going in," Emory said.

Contreras pulled him aside.

"I can help you. In the department. I know you're getting bored sitting behind a desk all day. You want to be chasing down ex-cons for the rest of your days?" Contreras asked.

"Part of the job... Don't fight me on this, Contreras. I like doing the right thing, the right way," Emory explained.

He proceeded to the door, but Contreras stopped him.

"Like tampering with evidence and signing off on cover-ups? I know a little bit about your past. You're no angel. You do me a favor and I can make that paperwork disappear," Contreras continued,

"If I take this Eddy Mack guy down, I'm bound for a promotion. I can bring you back in. You'll get your pension back and retire in honor with a badge,"

"What's so special about this kid?" Emory asked.

"Nothing, but he has an inside connection to Eddy Mack. We hold this over on him and maybe we can use him to help take him down," said Contreras.

"Mack? Alright... Make it happen," Emory said.

Emory handed Contreras Jimmy's paperwork before heading out. Contreras walked back in and waved the paperwork as he took a seat in front of Jimmy.

"These are your charges," Contreras said before tearing up the paperwork.

He continued, "Help me do something good. You'll walk out of here today."

Jimmy didn't even flinch. He didn't even say a word.

"You can work with me, get your shit together and start a new life, or you can go back to prison. Your call," Contreras said.

He pulled out his card and placed it on the table in front of Jimmy,

"This offer has an expiration date. Call me when you're ready to help yourself. You're free to go."

Jimmy stayed seated for a moment then looked down at the card. Contreras watched as Jimmy took the card and made his exit.

VI.

The shop was back to business as usual the next evening. Jimmy walked in through the front door and he was immediately greeted by Cody.

"Hey man, everything is kind of weird right now. Play it cool. No one knows you were here last night, so just be cool," Cody said.

Jimmy took off Cody's coat and quickly gave it back to him.

"Check on the restrooms. They need to be cleaned. After that, I'll show you how to work the phones." Cody said.

Jimmy went about his business and began gathering cleaning supplies from a storage closet. Cruz who was busy tattooing a customer was the first to notice Jimmy. Cruz gave him a dirty look. Eddy came walking out of the back room with a sketch design he wanted Cody to make a copy of. Eddy noticed Jimmy and greeted him.

"There he is! How are you doing today, pal?" Eddy asked.

"Not bad. Ready for day two."

"Cody is going to have you take calls and make appointments tonight," said Eddy.

Cody and Jimmy admired the sketch of a nineteen twenties roadster.

"Don't worry kid, we aren't training you to be a secretary. We may even break your cherry tonight if it's busy," Eddy said.

"Sounds good to me," Jimmy said.

Eddy walked back into the back room to start the tattoo. Cruz continued to work on a customer from his private stall. The customer was a twenty-five-year-old, Mexican gangster who noticed Jimmy cleaning. The customer reacted as if he was uncertain as to where he had seen Jimmy before until it finally hit him.

"Hey, ese, you see that vato over there cleaning?" The customer asked Cruz.

"The gringo?" Cruz replied.

"Chale, Holmes. I just got out of the county on a warrant, and I could have sworn I saw that vato inside."

Cruz looked over with a confounded look on his face.

"Is that right?" Cruz asked.

"Yup, that's him, ese."

Cruz sized up Jimmy again. A handsome and sophisticated man walked in through the front door. Cruz's twenty-four-year-old brother, Moctezuma. He sat next to his brother's stall.

"What's up, Cruzito? I wanted to ask you a favor," Moctezuma said.

Cruz took a moment to introduce his customer to his younger brother.

"This is my little brother, holmes."

The two exchanged a handshake.

"Mucho gusto, ese," said the customer.

"What's the word? I'm busy today," Cruz said.

"I wanted to see if you could lend me twenty bucks to go to a concert tonight," Moctezuma said.

Cruz motioned to the customer.

"This vato over here thinks he's going to graduate from college and changed the world," said Cruz.

"Well, it's better than being a gardener or a dishwasher," Moctezuma replied.

"Don't knock the hand that feeds you, ese. Dad was a gardener for years. That's the reason LA is so beautiful - Mexican gardeners," Cruz said.

They laugh. Hours later, Cruz was in front of the shop taking a smoke break. He noticed Estrella dressed in a tube-top and a mini skirt trooping up the sidewalk. She tried to walk past him, but he stepped in her path.

"I told you not to hang out around here," he said.

"I'm not coming here to see you," Replied Estrella.

She continued inside the shop.

"Where are you going?" Cruz asked.

Estrella walked into the main room and made her presence known immediately. She walked over to Cody as he finished wrapping the work in progress.

"Hi, Cody."

"Estrella, you can't be in here, your brother is going to flip," Cody said.

A furious Cruz put out his cigarette.

"He's not my dad, I can go where I please. I want a tattoo," Estrella said.

"No way," Cody said.

Estrella pulled out a small sketch of a rose from her purse.

"It's small. I want it on my ankle," she said.

Cody let out a sigh and shook his head. Cruz came storming in and grabbed Estrella by her arm then walked her through the back door as they shouted at one another. She slipped on her heel and fell to the ground when Cruz pushed her. She immediately jumped back up and slapped him across the face. Charged by adrenaline, Cruz grabbed her neck and pinned her against a wall. Jimmy noticed everything as he walked back from taking out the trash. He immediately pulled Cruz off of her. The two men went tumbling to the ground in an all-out brawl until Cruz produced a knife,

"You're a dead man."

"You think I'm afraid of a knife?" Jimmy said.

Cruz advanced with the knife but stopped when Eddy emerged from the shop,

"Cruz!" He looked at Eddy and immediately put the knife away.

"Cruz, come with me."

Cruz stared Jimmy down as he followed Eddy inside. Jimmy went to console Estrella. Eddy led Cruz into his office.

"I don't give a fuck about whatever is going on between you and your sister. I'm running a fucking business and I have zero time for this. This place got robbed last night and I'm sitting here with my dock in my hand, babysitting a fucking family feud. This is the last time we have this conversation," Eddy said.

"That pinche Guero is gonna die," Cruz said.

Eddy grabbed Cruz by his collar.

"You're not going to touch that kid. You do, I'll kill you myself. You're out of control," Eddy said.

"Did you know that the white boy was at LA county last night? I wonder for what? For all we know, he's the one that robbed us," Cruz said.

"You don't have any idea who sent that kid here, so shut the fuck up. You're taking the rest of the night off and I expect you to find the actual guys that stole from me so I can sever their fucking heads. Do I make myself clear?"

Cruz took a deep breath and gathered his composure.

"I got it," Cruz said.

VII.

It was dark out and Cody had finished closing up the shop by himself. A white van approached him as he emerged from the shop and locked the doors. Two men wearing all black leaped out and snatched him inside before the van sped away.

"Get the fuck off of me!" Cody demanded.

The men were in masks and proceeded to interrogate Cody.

"Shut the fuck up!" One of them screamed.

"Where's the shit?" Another one asked.

"I don't know what you're talking about," Cody replied before being punched in the face by one of them.

Another masked man grabbed Cody by his neck,

"If you don't have the shit then where is the money?"

"What shit? What money?" Cody asked.

"The heroin, muthfucka, where is it?" Cody stalled for a second.

"I'm sorry, guys. Right, of course, I think I must've misplaced it somewhere between fuck and you," Cody said.

One of the men choked Cody until he was out of breath. Another one grabbed both of Cody's hands and tied them to a wooden block,

"Smartass muthafucka... We'll see how you like boxing with no knuckles, chump."

One of the men produced a large hammer.

The next day Jimmy arrived at the shop well rested and in good spirits, but the only person around was Cruz.

"What's going on? Where is everyone?"

"The hospital. Cody got jumped last night," Cruz said.

A nurse guided Jimmy into Cody's hospital room where Eddy stood in distress. Cody was in a coma. Jimmy hugged Eddy,

"Thanks for coming. I just sent my wife and everyone else home to get some rest."

"How is he?" Jimmy asked.

"They're saying it's hard to know if he's gonna make it."

Jimmy turned to gaze over Cody as he laid in desolation,

"Who did this?"

Eddy didn't answer.

"I'll do whatever you ask me to do, Eddy. Just say the word and it's done."

The nurse walked in with a bouquet for Eddy. She handed him a personal envelope as well. 'For Eddy and Klein' the envelope read. He opened the envelope and read the card,

"I think we know who did it... When in doubt, have no doubt."

Eddy's eyes remained locked on the card as he crumbled it into the palm of his hand,

"I'm gonna hold you to that... You're with us now, Jimmy."

Eddy placed his hand on Jimmy's shoulder. It felt ominous. Cody was in deep sleep. Jimmy stepped outside of the room to make a phone call,

"Contreras. We need to talk."

Jimmy walked into Clifton Cafeteria to meet Contreras who was already dining in the corner of the restaurant. Jimmy sat down across from him,

"I heard about Eddy's kid."

"Who did it?"

"Have you thought about my offer?" Contreras asked.

"I'm not going to betray the one person who is trying to help me get a new start. I just want to know who did it," Jimmy said.

"I'm the one helping you get a new start," Contreras replied then continued.

"Look... right now, I'm sure it's just helping clean up around the shop. Next week, it's tattooing, but next month, it's armed robbery. Next year, who knows? Murder?"

"I've never killed anyone my country didn't ask me to," Jimmy replied.

"You don't know these guys. Half of those guys in that shop have rap sheets longer than you. Even Eddy's son."

"Cody... he's a good kid," Said Jimmy.

"Maybe, but when Eddy goes down and he will, the whole operation goes down with him. If he can't protect his son, where does that leave you," Contreras asked.

Jimmy was silent. Contreras produced a photo of Klein.

"Louis Klein-Herrera, a Mexican-Jew who grew up in Boyle Heights. He has an Ivy- League education, with a Fortune 500 mind. He owns one of the largest legitimate shipping companies in the country, but like most guys of that ilk, his vice is greed... He runs a trafficking organization through that very same business that delivers heroin and cocaine to distribution hubs in cities throughout the U.S. Not alone though. He has a little help from the Mexican-based cartels. Eddy Mack is merely one of his generals, albeit his most successful. Taking down Eddy alone would severely cripple the heroin trade in Los Angeles, but the end game is Klein," Contreras explained.

A waitress approached Jimmy, "What can I get you, darling?"

"I'm good," Jimmy replied.

Contreras, chimed in, "Get him a cup of coffee. Black."

The waitress walked away as Jimmy analyzed the photo of Klein,

"I've never seen or heard about this guy before."

"He's a psychopath," Contreras replied. He continued. "At least Eddy puts up the whole, 'serving his community' front. This guy doesn't give a fuck about anything but his money. Once he left the barrio, he never looked back."

"What is it you exactly want me to do?" Jimmy asked.

"I need you to gain everyone's trust. Keep me posted on the moves they're making. I need to know what they're gonna do next."

"Oh, now I get it," Jimmy replied.

Contreras took a moment to hide his frustration.

"I'm promising you a second shot at life, Jimmy. You were dealt a bad hand and I'm going to help you get that shot. Fast Eddy's is a dead end," Contreras said.

This landed on Jimmy. He took a sip from his coffee,

"No."

Contreras read Jimmy. Unsatisfied, he dropped some cash down.

"You're making a mistake," Contreras said.

"I didn't survive Vietnam and prison to become a rat. You should understand that," Jimmy explained.

Contreras looked over Jimmy once more. His expression changed to a look of disappointment. He exited the restaurant. Jimmy remained at the table, looking straight ahead, expressionless.

Echo & The Diamond

I.

A nineteen eighty-nine Harley Davidson FXR was cruising through a Las Vegas suburb. The gas tank read, 'The Diamond'. It was Sunday afternoon. A cross atop a church steeple reflected the blazing sun against a desert blue sky, dry August heat. A white bread wonderland. All around things were in bloom. Life was happening. People were happy. Lawns were being mowed, kids were jumping through sprinklers, cars were being washed, and young dogs walked old women.

"You probably thought this is where I lived, but if you did, you would be wrong."

The nineteen eighty-nine Harley Davidson turned into a gritty mobile home park. It passed a sign that read 'Aloha Vegas Mobile Home Park. Welcome, Home!' It was dilapidated with a broken muffler for the whole neighborhood to hear. Unlike the prior utopian wonderland, this place was an economically depressed area filled with weeds, rusting trailers, junked cars, and stray dogs. Night fell on a line of chromed-out Harley Davidson motorcycles parked in front of what appeared to be a well-kept single-wide trailer, but inside was a different story. Everything was in a state of packed or partially unpacked making for a strange moving box motif. Empty beer cans opened cans of Hormel Chili and Doritos bags were strewn across the kitchen counter next to used cigarette packages and loose change.

On an old, colored TV a televangelist prayed and urged the viewers to call the number on the screen and "sow a seed" so as not to "miss out".

The sounds of arguing, crying, overall emotional trauma come from behind a closed door. A large biker man who looked to be about thirty-four who was bearded and covered in tattoos walked briskly out of one of the rooms and zipped up his jeans before he threw on his leather jacket and headed for the door. He was followed and harassed by Trudy Jones who was thirty-two. White trash beautiful with a raspy voice, nice figure, lit cigarette in hand.

"This, however, was home. My mother."

Trudy shouted at the biker, "There you go again, you son of a bitch. Get what you want then go off disappearing. Bon Voyage, motherfucker! Bon Voyage!"

Trudy continued to pursue the man, still yelling and managing a decisive middle finger with her non-smoking hand. He exited and slammed the door in her face behind him. She stopped and trembled as she took a long hard drag and wiped a tear. With an open hand, she hit the wall before sliding down to the floor. Her head dropped between her knees. This was a pattern. She looked up from her nearly fetal position to see five-year-old Echo standing over her, staring with a blank expression, looking like she just woke up. The next night it was another random man who was asleep next to Trudy. He was more of a white-collar type than the last guy. Young Echo entered the room crying and holding a doll. Trudy immediately jumped out of bed to comfort her.

"Mommy, I can't sleep, I had a nightmare."

"Awe, sweetie. It was only a dream. It's okay. Everything is going to be okay," Trudy said softly.

She kissed young Echo on the forehead before the man called her back to bed.

"Get back over here. The little shit will be fine," He said.

Under the influence of drugs and alcohol, Trudy sent Echo back to her room.

"You'll be fine, baby. Mommy loves you."

Echo entered her bedroom which was not your typical teenage girl's room. She's a child of two worlds. An array of exotic weapons draped the wall. Old vintage photos of motorcycles from World War Two lasted on the ceiling above a bed with hand-sewn American Indian coverings. Numerous set-stills and international movie posters of the film, The Silence of the Lambs, graced the wall. Moccasins shared space with black biker boots on the shoe rack. On the tube was the film, The Silence of the Lambs. Clarice Starlings' FBI-issued Smith & Wesson model thirteen revolver was drawn on 'Buffalo Bill' in the final climactic scene of the movie.

"I must've watched her in that film a hundred times. I wanted nothing more than to be Clarice. Becoming a federal agent for the bureau was the only thing I ever dreamed of achieving in my life."

Life hadn't changed much for Echo over the years. She stood staring blankly at her fifteen-year-old self in the mirror before her. While the puffiness around her pale green eyes told the whole story, a storm still raged. In the reflection was the man's body which lied quietly behind where she stood with a pair of scissors in hand. She slowly began cutting large sections of her curly, blonde hair away from her lovely head. Careless cut after cut, leaving her looking otherworldly and waif- like. She took the lipstick from the make-up organizer on her desk and started writing on the mirror.

"Mom and I lived here ever since I could remember. Never met my father, but I sure did meet a lot of my mother's boyfriends, or just friends as she preferred to call them. After she was done having sex with whoever happened to be visiting for a sleepover that night, Mom would pass out drunk in her room, oblivious to the fact that her just friends loved making new friends of their own. In most cases, that would be me."

Echo remembers the moments before the man behind her fell asleep. He was holding her down by her arms on the bed. She was wincing and resisting, but to no avail. He moaned and thrust as he kept her locked in his grip, pressed down. That was before. This is now. She stepped over the man's dead body as she moved across the room. The memories still lingered. On the Native American style bedspread, the man's hand released one of Echo's arms and moved up to her neck. Is hand wrapped around it. Echo was in a panic as she gasped for air. A brief but clumsy balancing act on the footboard. Echo's free hand reached down by the side of her mattress and discreetly produced a nine-inch hunting knife. Tiny feet step off of the footboard and into space yet defy gravity. Spastic jerks in space. Legs hang still. The mirror caught a different angle. One with the man's body, but with the hunting knife protruding from the side of his neck. A sudden and utter stillness. A stream of urine flowed down black painted toes. In the mirror, the angle was now of Echo's hanging body next to the man's corpse and a message scrawled on the mirror in red lipstick that read, 'I am a fucking person.' EMS workers rushed into the room, checked on the man, and performed CPR on the Echo. As Trudy stood by, she wept and prayed. They revived the Echo.

II.

"I never wanted to take a life. Besides my own, that is. I don't know how many times I tried, but no matter how often, for some reason, it never worked. My grandmother was real religious and always used to tell me that God had a special purpose for me.

She used to say that nothing could take me out of here until I'd fulfilled my assignment on this earth."

Police read Echo her rights while she was on a gurney being attended to by EMS workers. A CSI worker exited the trailer holding the hunting blade in a clear plastic bag. A body bag was wheeled out of the trailer to a waiting coroner's vehicle.

"I should be brain dead, considering how long I was deprived of oxygen. I'm a miracle." Echo stood wearing an orange jumpsuit next to a public defender. A judge strikes her gavel. Echo stared straight ahead. Echo worked in a cafeteria kitchen and washed dishes at a juvenile correctional facility. "I started thinking that maybe my grandma was on to something."

Echo sat alone in the prison chapel with her head bowed. Suddenly she raised her head and her eyes popped open as if she'd received some sort of epiphany.

"So, I just decided to live."

Echo walked out of the prison carrying a bag of her belongings and a new lease on life. Echo was now nineteen. She practiced intensive training in a backyard. Sharpening defense tactics, fitness, and marksmanship with an air gun.

"As I got older, my determination and focus grew stronger. I also learned everything and anything I could about guns."

With an air gun in hand, Echo fired numerous rounds towards her given targets, with ease. On one target, pellets were indented within a small bullseye sphere. Her practice continued at a shooting range where she handled a Glock 9mm drawn on a set of Birchwood Casey paper targets. Every single shot hit the mark. Echo had developed an unmatched natural beauty.

"I wanted to be the best. Weapons would become a skill."

In a mixed martial arts academy, Echo practiced kata- a choreographed set of moves designed to deal with an imaginary attacker.

"Self-defense would become a preferred form of self-expression. My personal, visceral, expression of art."

Echo was twenty-one now. She sat at a desk in a full university classroom listening to a lecture.

"On the road to getting a shot at applying to the bureau, I would study criminal justice during the day and at night - well, it's Vegas, so you either work at a casino... or a strip club. Only, I wasn't planning on taking any clothes off."

On her desk was an MMPI2 test pack that read 'sample test.'

Echo's red nineteen ninety-four Geo Metro pulled into Jose's auto repair shop. The car sounded like a small Harley Davidson motorcycle which was evidence of a broken muffler. Echo rolled down her window and called out toward a stocky Hispanic man. The forty-eight-year-old shop owner was working on a car in the bay.

"Jose! Help a girl out. This thing's getting me dirty looks. What can you do for me, Hermano?"

Jose rolled out from under an old Buick wearing sunglasses,

"Hello, lady in red! What can I do for you?"

"This thing is too loud, Jose. Can you fix it for fifty bucks? How can you see under there with sunglasses?"

"I've been working on cars for so long, I already know where everything is under there. So, your muffler is not working. The part alone is going to cost around two-hundred. I can give you a break on labor, but you're still looking at around two-hundred to two-fifty. But I'm not free today. You can come by tomorrow, early- ok?" Said Jose.

"Oh, Jose... You're killing me. I'll see if I can come tomorrow, I don't know how I'm going to pull this off, but thanks," Echo said.

"Ok, is Echo. I save a spot just for you- eight o'clock," Jose said.

"Eight? On a Saturday?" She asked.

"Yep."

"Ok, you do that, Hermano. Gracias."

"No problem. You can speak English with me. To be honest I don't even know how to speak Spanish," Jose said.

Echo peeled out of the parking lot. In the seat next to her were an opened bank envelope and a letter. She looked down at it after stopping at a red light. It was a school tuition loan statement. Thirteen-hundred and fifty-four dollars was past due. She sighed and muttered under her breath.

"Shit."

III.

Various women from all walks of life filled a Moulin Rouge themed dressing room. A gorgeous and petite, twenty-two-year-old African-American woman named Katrina was putting on makeup against a classic Broadway-style vanity mirror. Beside her was twenty-year-old Maltese, who was counting a small pile of old, sweaty, crumpled up dollar bills.

"I'm not about to go twerkin' for some teenaged trust-fund kid flashing a handful of one-dollar bills, actin' like he's ballin'. I told you, them boys in the private dancing room? They got the money. You feel me?" Katrina elaborated.

"I guess I'm just a little shy," Maltese said.

"Girl, you ain't gonna get nothing in this world actin' shy. When you get off stage, you make sure those motherfuckers know you only do private dances," Katrina said.

Echo pulled up outside of the strip club, turning heads with her car's high decibel undercarriage audio output. This car was falling apart. Echo rolled down her window, reached her hand out, and opened the driver side door by pulling the exterior handle up. She exited as the valet approached.

"Hey man, sorry about the noise, muffler's broke. And she won't open from the inside, so you gotta roll down the window... to get out," Echo said to the confused valet.

"You know, driver side. Outside handle. To exit. The vehicle. Echo's patience was running out on this car and with people who just did get it.

"Oh... Ok. Got it. I think."

"You do. You got it," Echo said.

She handed the valet her keys and tried to hide an awkward combination of embarrassment and frustration. Echo approached the front entrance of the strip club. Her sexiness is undeniable in a pair of red cross-string knee-high boots draped over skin- tight leather pants. A bouncer met her at the door. Tall, overweight, and tattooed. He went by Leonard,

"New dancer?" The forty-four-year-old man asked.

"No. I'm working security tonight," she said.

Leonard smirked in disbelief,

"Here? With me?"

Katrina emerged emitting a high- pitched squeal at the sight of Echo before bear-hugging her from behind.

"Don't you wish, my friend! This is my best friend in the whole world that I haven't seen in forever, who is working inside with me tonight!"

Katrina said.

"Oh, girl! You look amazing! Thanks for hooking this up- oh my gosh, you look so good!" Echo said.

Leonard laughed as he unlocked the velvet rope and created an entry. Echo followed Katrina which gave Leonard a money shot of those tight fit leather pants.

"I see you, Kat. Ain't trying to mess with your stable. For the record, though with a body like that, your friend should be dancing," said Leonard.

"I used to tell her that exactly. Haven't seen her in two years. You still ain't lyin', though!" Said Katrina.

"You'll make more money, honey," Leonard said.

Echo held her ground and looked Leonard straight in the eye. Then finally reached out her hand to shake his.

"Name is Echo."

"Leonard. Good luck, princess."

"Sure," Echo replied.

Katrina walked Echo into Swifty's office for an introduction. He ran the joint. A fifty-nine-year-old who was a cross between a biker and a businessman. He sat at his desk playing with his cell phone.

"Swifty I want you to meet my best friend from way back, the one who's been studying to be a cop or whatever. I told you about her."

"The bodyguard?" Swifty asked confused.

"Personal security. But yeah. Nice to meet you. Echo Jones. I have my guard card right here," Echo said.

She reached out her hand to introduce herself and handed over the license to give him a better look at her.

"My goodness, you don't look like a security guard at all. Are you sure you wouldn't rather dance? You'll make five times the money. Hell, I'll give you a five-hundred-dollar bonus just to start," Swifty said.

"Thank you, but it's not my thing."

"Hey, Swift, the whole time I was in Europe, this girl's been hittin' the books- she don't mess around. Gonna audition for the F.B.I. Right, Ech?" Katrina said.

"It's not an Audi…"

Swifty cut in,

"Well, if that's what you want. Kat spoke very highly of you."

Intrigued by Echo, Swifty turned to Katrina and gestured with his head while lighting up a doobie.

"Have her start in the main room," he said.

Katrina made some space in her locker for Echo's belongings before she sat down to adjust her makeup. Echo bashfully sat her cheap, torn handbag next to Katrina's accessories, all high end, name brand. Louis Vuitton, Gucci, Chanel. Echo's Glock 9mm slipped out of her jacket and onto Katrina's lap as she went to hang it up.

"What the fuck?" Said Katrina.

"Oh shit. I'm sorry. Let me grab that," said Echo.

Katrina's face lit up,

"Girl! You're packing a gat? Can I hold it?"

Echo quickly grabbed the gun,

"No. I'm sorry. It's not a toy."

"Damn, you are a badass. Do you have it registered?"

Echo took out all of the ammo and handled the piece professionally before hitting the 'safety' lock.

"I need to get around to that. My grandpa gave it to me for my thirteenth birthday. I've just been..."

The music came in blaring when Maltese walked into the dressing room. She was carrying a handful of one-dollar bills, spoils of her just-completed stage dance.

"You're up next, Kat!" She said.

She noticed Echo,

"Oh hi! Are you a new dancer? I'm Maltese."

Echo was in game mode, trying to keep an eye on Katrina, who had disappeared to the bathroom to snort a line of coke.

"Like the dog," Maltese said.

"Oh. Hi. No, I'm working security. What did you say your-"

"Maltese. My gosh, you're so beautiful. I thought you were a dancer."

Katrina emerged from the bathroom, even more, energetic than before.

"Echo and I go way back. She may start dancing soon, but for now, she's here to keep the assholes in line," Katrina said.

Echo threw an incredulous glance at Katrina as she continued.

"And trust me, she's a badass. Future FBI agent."

Maltese got a bottle of Vodka out of her locker and started taking shots.

"Take it easy with that shit," Katrina said.

"It helps me take off the edge," Maltese replied.

Katrina spritzed some hairspray before heading for the backstage area.

"Just keep an eye on the pervs when they get up close. Don't let them touch me," Katrina told the Echo.

"I got you. Nobody's gonna touch you."

IV.

Flashing lights rained on Katrina as she did some acrobatic pole work before shifting into full-on twerk set during the music's chorus. The crowd went crazy as a Hispanic, tattooed thug moved in close about to slap Katrina's butt.

"Get back" demanded Echo as she swiftly came to her rescue.

"Get the fuck off me. Oh, wait, you fine, baby. What's your name? You wanna frisk me?"

"Just stay back," Echo said.

The man continued to harass Katrina as Echo returned to her post. She came back and placed the man in a sleeper hold before he knew what hit him.

"You were told," said Echo.

The rest of his crew of Hispanic males moved in to try and save him. Echo noticed one of them pull out a switchblade. She swiftly spun and landed a perfect roundhouse kick on one of the man's chin. The force spun the man before he fell to the ground out cold.

"Back the fuck off," Echo demanded.

The rest of the group complied and backed off. Leonard approached surprised and angry at the same time. Ready to throw the Hispanics out of the building. Echo looked up at Katrina and nodded with a thumbs up.

"You're good," Echo said.

Katrina flashed a sassy smile and continued her dance. Later, Echo and Katrina returned to the dressing room to find Maltese puking in a trash bin.

"Dammit, I told her not to drink so much," Katrina said as she rushed to help.

Echo grabbed some towels to hand to Maltese who leaned back, drained. It was obvious she was done for the night. Swifty ran into the room with a glass of water and headed straight for Maltese,

"I told you this girl was lush. I can't put her on stage like this."

Swifty produced some cash and turned to Echo,

"Darling, please! Look, I'll give you five hundred dollars cash-that's on top tips. I need a dancer. Please?"

Echo turned to Katrina who held the same question on her face.

"Five hundred dollars!" Katrina said.

Echo was considering the offer for a moment, but she balked.

"Fine, eight hundred dollars. I'm begging you," Said Swifty.

Echo realized that she would be violating her moral code but was also aware that quick cash like that would solve some real problems. She hit back at Swifty, which caught him off guard.

"A thousand. One thousand dollars."

He looked Echo over one more time. She drove a hard bargain, but there was something about this girl and he loved it.

"Tonight only," Echo said.

"Done. What do you like to dance to?" Swifty asked.

Just behind the stage, Echo was uncomfortable, but Katrina reassured her. The sound of impatient patrons emanated from the bar area. The girls couldn't help but laugh at this surreal situation as Swifty checked on them.

"What am I doing? This is crazy," Echo said.

"Don't worry, babe. the first time is always the hardest. But it's easy, just move your body to the music. You got this," said Katrina.

"Ready?" Swifty asked.

The crowded house began to holler displeasure at the empty stage. Echo took a deep breath before taking her first steps toward the stage. She emerged like a deer in the headlights but gradually began to find her groove. In light of Echo's striking beauty, her unpolished dancing chops were beyond forgivable, but she had that 'it factor', an intangible and unteachable 'presence'. After a moment Echo began to own the stage and come off as a pure natural. The crowd perked up and went wild. Men and women started to 'make it rain' with cash like never before. By the time the song was finished, the entire stage was covered in cash. Echo felt empowered in a way she never had before. She took heavy breaths and sweat glistened in the dusty light. The crowd was lit up with applause and cheers. The night was still young but satisfied now. Echo and Katrina waited for their respective rides out in front of the club. Echo clutched a transparent plastic bag she got from the kitchen. It practically overflowed with cash. Leonard's job description involved seeing to it that the women got into their vehicles safely. Katrina kissed Echo on the cheek and squeezed her tightly.

"You killed it, sister. Night!" Katrina stepped into her ride and blew Echo a kiss as Leonard closed her door.

She lowered her window. Echo blew a kiss back and raised the stuffed bag of cash.

"Maybe dancing is better... Night!" Echo said.

"You were doin' it all tonight, huh?" Leonard said.

"I don't know what I was doing tonight," Echo said.

"Could have fooled me!" Leonard replied.

Echo hollered at Katrina one last time as she rode off.

"Hey, don't forget! Brunch at eleven. See ya, hottie! I can't wait to hear all about Europe!" Leonard opened the door to Echo's ride.

She stepped in appreciating the courtesy, conceding to Leonard.

"But yeah, 'doing it all'. Goodnight. Thanks again," Echo said.

V.

Katrina and Echo splurged the next day at the Forum Shops at Cesar's Palace. They carried around bags that read Fendi, Louis Vuitton, and Gucci. The girls swiped credit cards without glancing at price tags. This wasn't the norm for Echo. Brunch at a nearby cafe, bottomless mimosas, croissants, smoked salmon, and fruit plates.

"What if I told you that the thirty-five hundred dollars, we just charged to this card were part of an allowance?" Katrina asked.

"What do you mean?" Echo asked.

"I mean it's not my card."

"You stole it?" Echo asked.

"No. I'm a lot of things. A thief isn't one of them. I'm a lady, first and foremost. I got the card from my Dang," Katrina explained.

"Your Dang? What exactly is a 'Dang'?" Katrina puckered up to break everything down.

"The simple definition of a 'Dang' or 'Sugar-Daddy' is someone who pays for sex or companionship. Otherwise known as a John, or a Trick. They can be found in casinos, hotel lobbies, gyms. Fangs have a certain look, and you can spot them anywhere. I earn close to twenty thousand dollars a week and that's not including shopping and travel perks - which, by the way, usually involve private planes and exotic locations. What do you think? You'll probably make more money than me."

Katrina finally finished rambling, Echo thought.

"You know, Katrina, stripping is already a bit of a stretch for a girl with plans to join the FBI. I can't"-

"-Girl, I already talked to Swift and everything is under the table at the club. No one will ever know that you worked at a dollar store."

"A dollar store, what?" Echo asked.

"Shake joint, skin bar, body shop."

"Oh, right. Well, for one Knight that was it, Kat. And this whole, 'dang' thing, I mean, that would be taking things to a completely new level. So, thank you, really, but it's... that's just... it's not me," Echo said.

"Well, when you change your mind, let me know. By the way, Swifty asked me if you want a spot tonight. It's a fight night, gonna be big bucks," Katrina said.

"You are trying to corrupt me, aren't you! Look, I'm doing your security as we agreed."

As the girls shifted back into a casual, friendly vibe, Katrina raised her mimosa glass for a toast.

"Yeah, we'll see. Here's to taking over the whole dang world," said Katrina.

"Here's to the world's foremost expert on how to be a persuasive, crazy bitch. Also, my best, lifelong friend in the whole dang world!" Echo said.

The girls threw their drinks back and laughed. This could be the start of something big. Later that night in the dressing room, Echo was trying to get a hold of Katrina on her cell to no avail. Swifty ran in frantically.

"Echo, I need you out front now."

"What?"

"I need you to take Katrina's place."

Two homicide detectives in their forties entered.

"Ms. Jones?" Detective Contreras asked.

"Yes."

"I'm Detective Contreras. This is my partner, Detective Floyd. We work homicide for the LVPD. Mind if we come in for a minute? We've got a couple of questions for you."

"Homicide?" Asked Echo.

She moved into a private room. The detectives followed her.

"Have a seat," said Contreras who produced a photo of Katrina.

Echo sat.

"Do you recognize this individual?" Echo is speechless.

"When was the last time you saw her?" Asked Floyd.

"I was with her all day today, what happened, what's going on?" She asked.

"Ms. Jones, Katrina Nesbit was found dead in her apartment about an hour ago," said Contreras.

Floyd noticed Echo's gun in her locker.

"We're going to need you to get dressed and come with us to the station for some questions," said Floyd.

"No. No, no, no. That's not possible. I just saw her. You have the wrong person. Her cell, I just called her cell, she..."

"I'm sorry, Ms. Jones," Contreras said.

"There's no... this isn't true."

Echo was so distraught that she appeared to start a panic attack. Her hands shook as she paced back and forth. Unable to process any of this, she hyperventilated. Everything seemed to go dark. Echo sat alone on a bench in a desolate residential park. She sat contemplatively as she recalled all that had happened over the last twelve, sleepless hours.

"We're still evaluating the bullet that struck Katrina."

She remembered hearing those words but didn't remember if it was Detective Floyd or Detective Contreras who spoke them. Katrina was shot dead. That's all that mattered.

"You can't join the bureau if you're a convicted felon."

Those were the words Detective Floyd spoke to her in the interrogation room at the LVPD. These were the words Floyd knew he'd speak the moment he saw Echo's gun in her locker.

"We have numerous contacts with the feds. We can make sure you have a clear path to the bureau and no skeletons in the closet blocking that."

Those were the gentler words of Detective Contreras. She was blackmailed but didn't put up much of a fight. She didn't have too much of a choice. On the other end of this assignment was the career she wanted. It would also bring purpose to Katrina's death because she wouldn't allow it to be in vain. Successful completion of the task would also prevent a lot of other Katrina's from dying.

"Sex crimes are at an all-time high in this town right now and we believe we have led to the head of one of the main operations behind it all. With your help, we believe we have a real shot at taking down these fuckers."

She didn't remember if it was Floyd or Contreras who spoke those words, but it didn't matter now. All that mattered now was that from this point forward she was undercover. The sun rose over Echo. She had almost forgotten the medium sized Fendi bag in her lap. Floyd had given it to her before leaving her alone on the bench.

"Inside the bag is detailed instructions. Where you will reside, what you'll drive, credit cards, bank accounts. Two cell phones are in the bag. The black phone is only to be used to contact me. Everything else is exclusively for the assignment," Floyd had told her.

A new day had dawned.

VI.

Her new name was Echo Mills. She learned this after having dumped out the contents of the Fendi bag Floyd gave her. It was the name on her new passports, bank cards, and license. She stood in the motel room she'd live in for the duration of the assignment. In North Las Vegas. It was a sun-faded, turquoise-colored old nineteen seventies style motel with rod-iron over the windows. The rooms were exactly what one would expect. Tacky sheets and covers turnover while an episode of 'Cops' played with poor resolution quality. One of the phones rang. She hesitated before answering. Before she could say hello, the raspy voice of a woman began speaking slowly with instructions,

"There's a diner across the street named, 'Sweet Sixteen' I'm sitting alone in a corner booth. Meet me in ten minutes. Bring what you need."

The woman was a large fifty-seven-year-old. She was stoic and naturally beautiful. She sat in the dimly lit diner with red vinyl banquette booths and Plexi countertops. She sipped black coffee out of an ivory porcelain mug as she observed Echo who entered and approached her table.

"Echo?"

"Yes."

The woman extended her hand,

"Hi, I'm Susan."

A tired, but pretty waitress approached.

"Can I get you something, Sweetie?"

"Black coffee is fine. Thanks," Echo said.

"Comin' right up."

The waitress left them. Echo sits.

"Listen, Hun, I'm not going to sugar coat any of this. We're going to be working deep undercover together," the woman said.

The waitress returned and poured the Echo's coffee.

"Tell me what I have to do," Echo said.

Susan waited for the waitress to leave then continued,

"You can call them whatever you want- tricks of the trade, Dangs, Joe Beasts, at the end of the day, they're all just predators involved with sex crimes."

Susan produced two photos. One was of a twenty-seven-year-old Middle Eastern man with excessive facial hair, with a unibrow, and slightly overweight.

"Arash Shayestah."

The other photo was of Miriam 'Phoebe' Sylvester. A fifty-five-year-old white female who was butch, rugged, and overweight.

"So, these are the suspects?" Asked Echo.

"In the flesh," replied Susan.

Echo stood nervously on the elevator at a cosmopolitan hotel on her way up to a penthouse suite. A private security guard stood post at the door. Large African American,

"Good evening. Can I help you?"

"I'm here to see Harold. My name is Misty," said Echo.

The guard opened the door without any hesitation. The room exemplified the pinnacle of exclusivity. Crystal encrusted wall textures, an unexpected art collection, and breath-taking views. Echo stopped to take it all in before an extremely handsome, debonair, and completely composed man approached her with a glass of champagne. Thirty-eight-year-old Dante Seravalli was not at all what she was expecting.

"Hello, my name is Dante, not Harold. It's a screening thing," Dante smiles.

He seems relaxed like he's done this a million times. To say he's charming, would be an understatement,

"What's your name?" P

"Well... the security guard thinks it's Misty, but I'm Echo."

"I guess we both have a screening process we adhere to. Rules of the game, I suppose."

"Is that what this is? A game?" Echo asked

"I'm not sure what this is, yet, but I like what I see."

"Ditto," said Echo.

Dante moved in closer and started to play with her hair.

"My gosh. You are stunning. Echo! That's an interesting name."

"My parents were hippies. Dante? You must be... Italian?"

"Straight off the boat! Second generation."

"Where are you from?" She asked.

"Philadelphia, originally, but I now reside in Los Angeles full time."

"I've never been to either. Born and raised in Vegas."

"Really? How would you like to visit L.A. tonight?" Dante asked.

"What do you mean?"

"I have to fly out to pick up my dog from the vet in the morning. We'll come back tomorrow afternoon, just in time for lunch."

Echo stalled to think about this unexpected proposition.

"I'd love to see LA! How would we get there?"

"We'll be boarding my Gulfstream!"

"A boat?" Echo asked.

"Airplane. Private jet,"

Echo looked bewildered and excited at the same time. On the Gulfstream Six, tucked away in the back corner of the cabin, Dante and Echo kissed passionately under a luxurious travel throw. It was obvious that their chemistry was real. After a day filled with shopping Echo and Dante relaxed in the tub of a presidential suite while listening to soft music.

"Today was magical. The last twenty-four hours have been unbelievable. You know how to spoil a girl."

They both took lines of coke before making passionate, amazing love in the bedroom. Morning came and Echo was woken from a deep sleep by a hard knock on the door. She looked around, but Dante was gone. It was just her and her Beverly Hills shopping bags. Echo moved slowly toward the door and opened it gingerly. On the other side were Susan and Detective Floyd. They instructed her to keep doing what she was doing and warned her to not get caught up in the drugs. They were closer now to cracking the case. Echo needed the reminder. She was looking for the man who murdered her best friend, but she was side-tracked. She was instructed to go see Arash again. By now she was able to just knock and walk into his hotel room. They've established a mutual trust for one another. Echo arrived at his hotel where Arash sat on the couch as he took bong hits, snorted cocaine, and played Call of Duty.

"How are you?" He asked Echo as she entered.

"Great, thanks to you! I appreciate you setting me up with Harold!"

"Oh, the guy is a whale! He'll take good care of you if you take care of him," Arash said.

"Tell me about it. He already took me on his private jet."

"Dante is a minor league. Just wait, I have another Dang I want to set you up with tonight. He'll be in town from New York until this weekend. He owns half of the real estate in Manhattan," Arash said.

He produced his phone and showed the Echo a photo of the guy. Mason Farrow was handsome and debonair. In the photo, he stood between two models in their twenties. Echo was shocked to see that one of the models was Katrina. She quickly shifted back into character.

"Where is he staying?" She asked.

"He likes Cesar's for some reason. He wants two girls so I'm going to send you and another new girl," Arash said.

"Can it be me and Lisa? Please?"

Lisa was a comedian Echo has clicked with during the assignment. She's one of Arash's regulars. They've become like sisters.

"I'm not sure he'll like Lisa," Arash said.

"Please? I feel comfortable around her, especially if this dude is kinky."

Arash took another bong hit.

"Alright, just make sure Lisa goes easy on the partying. She's no good if she does too much coke," Said Arash.

VII.

Echo was in her motel room cleaning her gun. On tv was the Silence of The Lambs. Clarice's reactions to Hannibal Lector's Florence Italy monologue. Echo stockpiled ammunition while at the same time took brief moments to focus on her favorite character. She remembered wanting to kill Arash the moment he showed her the photo of Mason Farrow with Katrina. It was enough that Arash was a part of all of this shit and in her mind, it would've been justified, but she knew she had to be smart. She wanted to kill them all, but she had to start with Mason. Echo turned off the tv, lights and exited the room. Echo sat at a bar drinking a Coca Cola waiting for Lisa to arrive.

"Sooty, I'm late," said Lisa.

"You're not late."

"Ok, well it felt like I was late. I've been running around town all night. I got great news!"

"Tell me! Tell me!" Said Echo.

"I'm signing with a comedy agent tomorrow. A guy came to the club last night and loved my set. He gave me his card and wants to sign me! I checked him out online and he's super legit!" Lisa said.

"Oh my gosh, Lisa that's amazing, congratulations! When do we celebrate!?"

"Let's go out and have a nice dinner this weekend. Just the girls!" Lisa said. "Sounds like a plan, girl!"

"So who's the other guy we're meeting tonight? What's the story?" Lisa asked.

"This one is easy money. He doesn't even want sex. Arash said he gets off by just having girls dance naked for him," Echo explained.

"Works for me! How much?" Lisa asked.

"Five thousand each for the night."

"I guess we're going shopping before dinner then, to celebrate!" Lisa said.

"Works for me!" Echo said.

They shared a laugh. Both enter the Cesar's Palace villa where Mason is dressed to impress with meticulous detail and an obsession with cleanliness. His grooming was immaculate, and he had an air of elegance that could be noticed from a distance.

"Good evening, ladies."

Lisa took the lead as she seemed to like Mason,

"Hello, handsome!"

"Hi," Echo said plainly.

"Come inside, make yourselves comfortable. Ladies, I'd appreciate it if you wouldn't mind taking off your shoes first."

Both girls do as they're told. Mason pours them expensive wine before all three moves to the white leather couch.

"For the record, you two ladies are sexy as fuck. I'd love it if the two of you would remove all of your clothing."

They adjust to the awkwardness and adhere to the instructions.

"Slower, slower don't be in such a rush."

"Do you have any coke?" Lisa asked.

Mason got up and moved to the grand piano where he prepared a few lines on a square mirror.

"Do you like blow?" Mason asked.

"If you give me blow, I'll give you a blow," Lisa giggled.

Mason took a second then smirked.

"I'd rather just sit here and watch you two get it on."

Echo partook as well. The music intensified and the girls pretended to kiss but didn't quite go there. Mason brought out a bag of dominatrix toys for the girls to play with. They go along with it. Later in the living room area, Echo woke right before noon. Partially nude and hungover. As soon as she regained her lucidity, she looked around the room only to notice that she was all alone. She panicked. The phone linked to Detective Floyd was missing. She grabbed the other one and called Lisa, it went straight to voicemail. Echo frantically grabbed her things and slipped out through a rear veranda door. Back at the cosmopolitan hotel Echo banged on Arash's door until he answered.

"What the fuck?" He said.

Echo didn't reply before storming past him,

"Where's Lisa?"

"What do you mean? I thought she was with you," Arash said.

"She was with me last night, then I woke up in the Dang's hotel at Cesar's, and they were both gone.

"They're probably at the pool or something. Relax," he said.

"No. You fucking relax. All the dude's shit was gone. Hers too. Like he checked out of the hotel."

"Let me just call the guy," Arash said.

He did and Mason's cell went straight to voicemail. Arash continued,

"Listen, I have an appointment. Just go home. Take a bath. Relax. As soon as I get in touch with them, I'll call you, okay?"

"Call me as soon as you get in touch with them," Echo demanded.

She had arrived back at her hotel, but before she could reach the main entrance an FBI Charger pulled up in front of her. Two federal agents hopped out of her vehicle and flashed their badges. Luke and Dana.

"Ms. Templeton?" Dana asked.

"Who are you?" Echo asked.

"We're the FBI and we need you to get inside of the vehicle."

Echo was amazed, scared, and excited all at the same time.

VIII.

Echo sat in an interrogation room bewildered as she was forced into questioning.

"We understand that you struck a deal with Las Vegas Homicide?" Luke asked.

"Detective Floyd and a woman named Susan. I thought she was a cop too," Echo answered.

"Well, both of those individuals are off the case now and the FBI is stepping in. You'll be working with us now," said Luke.

"Criminal Justice graduate with honors. Very impressive," Dana continued, "We know about your aspirations to join the FBI. Dreams do come true."

"How? By giving some old pervert a hand job?" Echo asked.

"Let's just say, if you help us, we'll help you," said Luke.

"You help us take these scumbags down and I guarantee you a trip to Quantico," said Dana.

"Do you think Farrow is the person that killed my best friend Katrina? I found a picture of her taken with him and now my friend Lisa disappeared with him as well. Is Lisa dead too? Did this motherfucker kill Katrina?"

Echo let everything out and broke down.

"These are all possibilities with Farrow. He's a psychopath and has no remorse for humanity. He litters used a 'rough sex gone wrong' defense and got away with murder last year. This little sex ring that you've gotten yourself involved in is full of unstable people suffering from mental impairment, perversion, lust, greed, addiction, and evil. There's been a plethora of STD epidemic spreading in this town along with missing persons and unsolved homicide cases- all of which are centered around prostitution, sugar daddy arrangements, escorting, danging- whatever you want to call it," Dana explained.

"So, what do I do?" Echo asked.

"Let's stick to the same cover and remain close to Arash Shayestah," Luke said.

"The phone. Either Farrow or Lisa- one of the two might have the phone that was given to me by Detective Floyd."

Echo wrote down the number on a piece of paper. Agent Luke took it.

"Helpful. We'll be in touch," he said.

Echo arrived at Arash's hotel room only to find him dead. While she sped down the highway fifteen miles over the limit on the diamond she had been involved in an accident. It didn't stop her from reaching the federal building where she sat in front of Luke and Dana all beat up.

"You're lucky to be alive," said Dana.

"Arash wasn't so lucky. It was an overdose that took his life," Luke added.

"Are you doing drugs?" Dana asked.

"You're kidding right?" Asked Echo.

"You just totaled your motorcycle on the highway. It's a miracle you're even still alive. Not a fucking scratch," said Luke.

"Cocaine. Fucking cocaine," Echo said.

"How long?" Dana asked.

"Ever since I got thrown into this," Echo replied.

"We know you're on our side, but it has to be all the way," Dan said.

"I swear I'll never use drugs again. I was undercover and in too deep, but I vow to never use it again. That's a promise," Echo said.

Luke and Dana looked at one another. They desperately wanted to believe Echo. Luke got an important text.

"We have a location for Farrow. He's in Boulder City," Dana and Luke scrambled to gather the essentials including loaded guns before leaving.

Luke gave Echo a loaded gun and an FBI jacket before they all scurried out.

IX.

A two-hundred-acre lot on the outskirts of town was filled with garbage and recycled items. Mason Farrow was cracked out as he operated the bulldozer that shuffled the trash and the remains of Trudy Jones' dead body. With him was Lisa who sat terrified, tied up, and gagged. Mason sipped a Budweiser while listening to loud music as he operated the vehicle. He stopped and got out where a Ford F-250 was parked. He moved to the bed and took up a blow torch, meat hooks, and trash bags. Next, he untied Lisa from the passenger seat of the bulldozer and yanked her out. He drags her to a portable conveyor machine where he tied her arms. She was petrified. Unable to scream or speak. An FBI helicopter appeared and hovered over the lot. The pilot gave coordinates to Luke who had driven through mountains of trash in search of Mason's truck. With him were Dana and Echo. He slammed on the breaks at the sight of the Ford F-250 and demanded that Echo remain in the truck. He leaves her behind even despite her protest. Luke and the other agents are met by Mason, who emerged holding two guns. One was pointed outward and the other was pointed at his torso.

"Go ahead and shoot me!"

"Put down your weapons!" Luke shouted.

Dana and additional agents showed up to provide back up.

"I'm high on methamphetamine!" Said Farrow.

"Put the guns down!" Said Luke.

He tossed one of the guns toward the agents but kept the other aimed at his torso. He seemed to be slowly calming down. Possibly even near surrender. Echo slowly emerged from the van and inconspicuously moved toward the action with her gun in hand. She can see the standoff from afar, but Lisa was nowhere in sight. She continued to survey the area until her eyes locked in on Mason's truck. A worker on the lot emerged and motion Echo over to something he had discovered. He too didn't want to interrupt the standoff, but unbeknownst to him, he would be calling Echo over to find the remains of her own mother's body. Echo maintains a principled facade as she jogs over with her gun held low then immediately breaks down in disbelief. She moved in close to Trudy's corpse and conveyed her love for her mother, only now it was too late. After a moment, Echo found the strength to recompose herself before getting the ultimate revenge on Mason. He seemed like he was calm now, but he quickly produced a syringe and proceeded to inject himself with meth. The gun was now placed at his feet.

"I'm shooting up meth! Stand back or else!" He screamed.

The agents advanced as Mason became more belligerent and confrontational. Echo moved in on Mason's truck and discovered Lisa tied up near a slab track. At that moment, Mason had stepped away from the agents and dashed around a corner and noticed Echo who had untied Lisa. He rushed and grabbed the blow torch then aimed a flame at the girls. They backed away as the conveyor machine ignited. Luke and the agents caught up to Mason, but the damage was done. The flames were out of control. Luke fired at Farrow and missed. Mason tossed the torch and picked up his gun. Luke rushed Mason in a panic but tripped. He was now an open target for Mason's gun which was aimed directly at his head. Before Farrow could pull the trigger. He was hit by multiple rounds. He fell to the ground dead. Echo was right on target and didn't miss a shot. She untangled Lisa and removed the duct tape as Dana and the other agents arrived. Echo and Lisa embraced out of pure love and relief. Dana walked over to the girls to assist Lisa to an ambulance for immediate convalescence. Luke slowly got up with assistance from Echo.

"You saved my life," he said.

The next day Luke and Dana waited for Echo outside of the McCarran International airport. Out of a convoy of cars, the sounds of Thunderheader pipes roared as Echo who was riding the diamond slowed to a stop. She removed the helmet. This was her mother's bike, and she made a promise that they would live through one another wherever she goes.

"I'm going to miss you both," Echo said.

Luke handed Echo her airline ticket.

"What are you going to do with the motorcycle? You're boarding a plane in a couple of hours," he said.

"I'm not going to need a ticket," Echo replied.

"You're going to ride out there aren't you?" Luke asked.

"Don't worry. I'll make it in time for day one," she said.

"Suit yourself," said Luke.

Luke moved in for a hug, something totally out of his character.

"Be careful," he said.

All three shared a moment. Echo and the diamond road through the picturesque roads of Virginia. A new day had dawned. One thought remained.

"Dreams do, come true, but the work has just begun on the long road to avenge evil."

And now these three remain: faith, hope and love. But the greatest of these is love. Corinthians 13:13

THE END

www.ingramcontent.com/pod-product-compliance
Lightning Source LLC
Chambersburg PA
CBHW050739180626
46814CB00002B/825